Other books by Jean Marie Rusin

Spooky

Willow Lakes Hauntings!

Mysterious Nights séance ghostly hauntings!

Poison Pen Pal

A Polish Christmas story with a magical Christmas tree

Broken Bridge Lies Body of water

Thin Ice Zombies In LA Nowhere to runs or hide! (RETURNS)

Thin Ice Zombies IN LA Nowhere to run or hide!

Detour

Night of Terror

A Drama queen collide with Prince Charming!

No Ending Dreams

No Ending Dreams (Reunion)

No Ending Dreams (Secrets)

Thin Ice Zombies In LA Nowhere to Run or Hide!

BATTLE

Jean Marie Rusin
Edited by K. D.

authorHOUSE®

AuthorHouse™
1663 Liberty Drive
Bloomington, IN 47403
www.authorhouse.com
Phone: 1-800-839-8640

Published by AuthorHouse 2/24/2012

ISBN: 978-1-4685-5575-2 (sc)
ISBN: 978-1-4685-5574-5 (e)

CONTENTS

Battle Continue 1

Alive 6

Zombies Part 2 10

Darkness Rise! 14

"Antidote Side Effective" 17

"You Save Me" 20

Mayhem And Death Part 2 23

Battle Zombies And Vampires!!! 26

Vampire's Territory 29

"Zombies World" 33

Flu Shot Went Wrong! 36

Trapped Between Zombies And Soldiers 39

Night Of The Living Dead Part 2 43

Time Running Out 47

Out Of Control 50

Thin Ice Zombies 53

Contagion Spreads! 57

Contagion Day 1 58

Contagion Day 2 61

Contagion Day 3 64

Epidemic End 67

Experiment Procedure 70

Zombies In Dark Tunnel 73

Tattoo Girl Trapped Around The ZombiesNo Escape From Them! 77

In The Middle Of Zombies 78

Revenge 81

Walkers 84

Zombie In Love 87

Lost 91

Terror In Paradise 95

Dark Territory 98

The Red River 101

Open Water 105

Rescuing Kelly At Sea 108

Under Siege 111

Solar Flares 114

Meteor Showers 117

Campsite 120

"Haunting" 125

Dark Shadows 126

House Of The Dead 129

Follows By The Undead... 131

End Of The Road 133

Volcano Erupt Lava Flow 137

Volcano Erupt 138

Cemetery Of The Dead, Coming Back To Live......... 141

President And His Family Attack In The White House Part 2 144

Bringing Out The Dead 148

City Of Dead 151

End Of The Line.. 154

Full Moon 157

Morning Sunlight 160

Zombies Are Coming!!!.. 163

Humans And Zombies.. 166

The Walking Dead 170

Walkers, Everywhere We Turned 174

Quarantine Part 1 181

BATTLE CONTINUE

We arrival to Los Angeles and we came to the shore and landed near the dock, and then we saw the zombies approaching us and so I told Tina and Kelly we need to leaves now, so we hurried to get back to boat and sail away and didn't looked back, so where will we go and Kelly said I don't know, Tina. But hold on tight and Kelly put the full power on the boat that Tina almost fell into the water, and Tina started to call Kelly names and said Kelly said I will navigation where we will go! Yes and we probably be eaten up by zombies, well I don't like how you are acting and you don't trust us, I don't, in my eyes I just sees how you killed my son Brain, and I don't know why you killed him? Well he became to be a zombie and I had no choice so I did kills a zombie and not your son. I don't understand your knowledge, but that the ways I survive. I guess so but I will not argue with you anymore and then Roger said that is a relief and now we can sail peaceful, yes. But where are we going I think to Australia, down and under and you think that we will be freed from zombies, that I don't have a answers but we are in the pacific ocean and we will be passing Hawaii and then China and then heading to Australia, well I never been there before, but we will be far, away from home that is true and I also I can check out if the infection spread, there!

Says if it did and then what will we do? I don't know but I think we will be fine and I safe for awhile... we will stay there and then we will have to sail away but if we are invaded by zombies and we will not be safe no place, that is true, so if you sees any of them coming, so runs has fast has you can. Remember run to the boat and get on and then started it up and if you don't sees us just leaves, I don't know how to navigation the boat, and how to sail, I were gets lost in sea, probably you were get lost

1

but maybe not, and not sure but you need to be ready to be on your own, but you are saying that you would leave me, no but ready to know how too survive, well I always had my son and now I am alone but you have us and but in some case that we separate so you need to know what to do and then Roger said she is right and I will not disagree with her. Well I hope that you won't abandon me? No I will not. Promise me, that I cannot do, things do happened and I cannot explain it but you need to be ready, yes. Listens too me said Kelly, I will looked around and I am coming around and then looks around but we would able to walks deeper and deeper into the woods and now I knew that were safe from zombies I thought, at that time! Roger and Tina and I walk and walk far from the beach and then we saw a lot of houses and said where rest of the residents of this city is? I don't know, maybe they are inside having lunch. But it is really quiet here and I just have a bad feeling and I think that we should walks back to the boat and sails away, are scare, Kelly? Yes, I am and I think we should go now!!! No, we are going too looked around and see what going on here, well if you don't know how, but this place is infestation with zombies and don't you feel death and sorrow here? No your imagination is playing tricks on you, no it is not, and now you are just being in a panicked and you also have fear and think the worst, but this place seem like it will be ours home now. Now you are telling us where we will lives, yes because you don't understand what I am saying. I am not crazy and I sure do know what I am doing, just leave me alone, Tina, fine and I am going to knock at the door and those nice peoples will let me in, now I know your out of your Mind, Tina. They can be infection and the worst they could be zombies, why the worst scenario, I really don't like your character lately, why but I am telling the truth and you are not listening too me, are you? Stops argument and gets along, so why do we have to listens too you, Roger? That is a good point so I am going to knock at this door and so if you wants to hide out in the bush that is fine with me, so I will hide out with Roger and be careful, sure I will! Tina went up too the door and knocked and then she opens the door and it was a lady but like stumble on her feet and Tina said are you ok? Then Tina notice the drooling and vomit on the floor and Tina said sorry too bother you, so I will go leaves and then the lady grab her arms and Tina started to yelled out and out of the bushes, Kelly and Roger, came out and rescue, Tina and said Kelly too Tina, I told you so.. But you don't have says it, I know, thanks for saving my life, once again, said Kelly. Don't rub it in and I just don't wants to talked about it anymore and I just wants to leaves this awful place, I don't where we go and it is infestation with zombies and I think that we will stay here for while. But we will have to deal with the zombies and I don't like it but it here and there in the states it will be the same, don't you gets it, yes I do but I don't feel right about this place, I don't neither but, we are staying, Kelly and Roger and but Tina was not happy about it not at alls. Tina walks toward the shore and Roger and Kelly said that we should be together and not separate, yes and we need to follow her, ok, I don't like that you are so pushing, I am not! Seems like you know what going on and you are not telling us. I probably do and so but I will protect you and Tina, so what happened if something happen too you, it won't how do you know, I just do. You must know more than you are saying, yes you right! But silent, do you hears something, yes I do I wants to listens, oh no! They are coming!! Who? The zombies and they are very hungry and they want our brains… that not good. I agree and so be quiet and they are very near and I think that Tina been caught… and we need to save her once again!! Not again!! so they walks very slowly and then they saw zombies have Tina and we need to distract them and get her away from the zombies, I have no clue, but that is not good for Tina, but she left us and we told her too stays. But we need to save her and I don't want her to dies, she won't! I got a plan, and we won't get killed neither, good plan. But we need to figure out how keep her out trouble, and we will I will watched her like a hawk.

Who will watch you, I will be fine, I am not that sure about that Kelly, she goes and doesn't tell us and then she get into trouble I know that Roger. Once again Tina, walks ahead and leave them behind and then Tina bump into Will and said who are you and how get you get here? Well we came here by boat, so I want to leave this place, so we can meet up and leave this terrible place. I agreed, so follows me, I will. They walk back, then she looked at him, he sounded, strangely, what wrong with you?

Nothing, are you sure? Yes but you are shaking and fell down to the ground, and pick him up, and he was not the same has he was and now Kelly knew that Roger was infection by the virus and he has 24 hours before it hit him badly. Will said to Tina that we should aboard the boat before it is too late, but I need to gets my friends and then we can leave do you understand. No, we are going and we are going to leaves them no I am not, we are going back to gets them, because Roger has the keys to the boat, ok I will grab the key and I will run to the boat and you follow me, I am not going to abandon my friends. We cannot stay here because the zombies are coming and we will be "dead meat" but I am not going to leave my friends neither, fine! Meanwhile Kelly and Roger don't trust

Will and Tina is not that smart, I know. But we need to warns her not too trust him but she will not believe what we says. I know but you need to get through too her, I will, thanks! But what do I says too her and not too defend her and not get her mad, well you need to be smooth and not means and nice too to her but why, every time she does something she get herself into trouble, so she is that type of person, don't you get it? I do and you making me sick of your whining, so I am not a whiner. Tina walks away and called out Will, I am just going to leave them, are you sure? So let go, and Kelly and Roger would following. Are you saying that they are catching up to us? Then Tina looked at Will and you are a zombie, no I am not! Then she shown he a mirror and he saw his face and he knew that he was a zombie and said when did it happen? I don't know, but I have too killed you, no you don't!

Ands you are following zombies and probably would take you to the rest of the zombies and you were being dead. What are you saying? Well you are probably stupid and you trust peoples and I don't know but you are clueless and you would end of dead if Roger you would be zombies and that is pitiful, thanks a lot and I don't wants to talks with you right now. I will follow Will and it is not a trap, well you dumb and stupid and you want to end being dead. So it is fine, and I won't repeat myself again! But Roger and I are staying here and I think that we will find a way home and that we won't have to fight with the zombies anymore. Tina follow Will to the boat dock and was about to step inside and then she saw that she was surrounded by the zombies and Tina said I trusted you and you betray me, well I am a zombie and your friend was right about me.

I don't know what to do but I cannot stay with him and I will become zombies and then you will have too shot me. Then I will be dead and then I will not be able to sees my family and that is a terrible thought and I don't wants that, well if you are infection, and you will become one and then I will need to shoot you, I don't wants to hears that! " Will please don't bite me, I don't want to end up dead, but I am hungry for brains and you are standing next me and about one minute later, Kelly ran up to her and said to Will I don't wants too killed you but you are a zombie and then she shoot him in his head and the head flew all direction and landed in front of Tina and she was alls in blood and she said I need to wipe off the blood and I don't wants to be infection, you won't, did you get any in your mouth, I don't think so! I need to know, if you get infection I will shoot you and you will be dead, ok, I got the message so let go back to Roger.

Kelly called out and said Roger where are you? But no sight of him and now Kelly was getting really worried about her friend Roger. " Then Roger walks up and said looked at her, she is a mess and her clothes are alls in blood and did she gets any blood inside of her and we need to quarantine her and locked her up, Tina said I refuse too be locked up and I am not infection with the virus, so how do you know? I don't but I will be fine, don't let him locked me up because then the zombies will gets me. You need to listened to me we need to gets off this island because it is swamps with zombies and we will dies. Roger said her mind is affect. "Don't listens to him he never likes me so, he wants too gets rid of me and that is not true, Kelly said. Tina walks very slowly and when they got near to the shed, Tina ran off and Roger ran after her and somehow she got to the boat and took off the anchor and started up the motor, and then Roger said shit, shit, shit, and what will I tell Kelly she will be pissed with me.

Tina screamed out and said "you bastard hope that you rot in hell" and then sail away from the island and then Tina saw the zombies in the water and now what will I do? And they were coming closer and closer too her. Tina thought to herself should go back, no I am going to beat those zombies and I will be dead meat, and there food supplies.

Tina kept on sailing and thought she was safe and about a moment later, about five zombies were on the boat with her and she didn't notice it until they were standing right next too her, oh my god! Tina tried to get off the boat but they were also in the water, and she was trapped and without a weapon to kill them, then they approach her and fight with them but the battle was being won by the zombies. Then Kelly ran downstairs and locked the door and then there was a banged and they were inside and the boat hit the rock. Somehow Tina fell into the water and saw there was a island and got off and ran for her life and didn't looked back, about two hours later, Tina was hiding in a cave and scare.

ALIVE

Tina was barely alive and difficulty walking and was about to passed out, but she find a cave and Tina had a lot of bruises and cuts and blood dripping from her body, and Tina didn't know how to stops the blood and in pain. Meanwhile Roger went back to Kelly and Kelly said where she is? She took off on the boat and how could you let her go? Now we are stranded on this island and we are going to dies. No we are not I saw a boat on the other side of this island and I think that we would not be caught by zombies and able to leave this island and about Tina, well don't worry about her she left us and without a boat and probably half ways home and she didn't care about us and why are you worry about her well I just have a bad feeling about her, just forget about her and let walking on the other side and find that boat and let hurried before it gets dark, ok I won't think about it anymore! Meanwhile at the cave Tina use her flashlight and then she looked around but the bleeding was severe and Tina didn't know how stops the bleeding then she looked into her pant pocket and use a lighter and burns her skins and it stop the blood.

Then she once again looked around and started a fire to keeps warm and sat down and she somehow had a pillow and then she decided to lay down and she thought she was safe but then she fell asleep and then they came inside and surrounded her and but she was fast asleep and then suddenly she woke up and the zombies were around her. At that moment Tina was weak and was unable to get up and Tina was afraid if she did, the bleeding would start again, but also Tina didn't wants to get bitten but also thought of dragging herself on the ground but then she knew that she couldn't go out the same ways has she came in so she decided to go deeper into the cave but she was still surrounded and she knew this time

6

she probably were died, so Tina just thought but they approach her and now she knew that she were be eaten by the zombies and she knew that she should have stay with Roger and Kelly.

About a minute later, they caught Tina and torn her apart and the blood spatter and bodies parts were all over and they were chewing her, and pulling out guts and liver and heart and her brain.

Meanwhile Kelly and Roger had a lot of obstacle but they were not going to give up and get back home, and Kelly said "are we going the right way"? Yes it is over that mountain across that river, I don't like this. But why? I don't k now, we are being follows by the zombies, I hope that you are wrong Kelly, I think that I am not and we must hurried, and I really mean it and I am not joking around they are very close too us. But we are not too far from the boat, in five minutes we will be there, are you sure? Good and I cannot wait to get off this Zombies Island, I agree with you, Kelly.

Then they got there and they saw about one hundred zombies and now what? We need to distract them and get to the boat and sail away! So who will distract them, you, I said Roger? Yes Roger you are a man and you will be able to fight them off and then we boat could leaves this terrible place, ok, I will get too the boat and I will started up and then I will find a flare and firing it at the zombies and you runs for your life too the boat and then we can sail away from this terrible place, I do agree that should work and I hope so, I don't wants lose anyone else. Kelly ran to the boat went Roger started to fight and then Kelly shot the flare up in the air and Roger ran to the boat and then they sail away and Roger and Kelly were relief for a moment. But looked they are in the water, no I don't believe this but we need to full throttle and hit a few zombies and get the hell out of this area and get back to LA, and about ten minute later they saw Tina boat broken into pieces and said well I guess she is dead and she didn't wants to stayed with us, so I tried to explained to her but now she is dead. I don't wants to talk about her and then the boat stall in the middle of the ocean and then Kelly said, now what are we going to do and Roger said well I am going to fix the engine and we will get out of here, do you how too fix it? No, but I will tried, fine but hurried, why? Don't you sees the white sharks circles our boat, and then a moment later, don't sees the zombies also in the water and we need to move now, do you have a paddle and then we can move, so Kelly you paddle and I will work on the engine, and then Kelly, I am a bit thirsty and hungry well that I cannot help because I also hungry and thirsty, so paddle and shut up! Kelly was paddle the boat and then got tired and the boat just was going further and further in the ocean and drift into unknown location and Kelly said I don't know where we will end up but I am too weak to paddle and Roger said don't worry, I will check it the radio working, and then I can called the coast guard and then we can get rescue, but please work on the engine and then I will try the radio and do a "SOS" good. Meanwhile the sharks were circles the boat and zombies were not too far from the boat and then, Roger and Kelly just sat in the boat for days and days. I think they don't see us but the sharks are not leaving, SH! Ok, I will be quiet and then, the storm came in and it started to pours and thunder and lighting, and the wind came in and Kelly and Roger, I don't what going to happened but hold on tight and don't let go! I won't!

At that moment seems like the boat was about too tip and Kelly said don't fall into the water, hold on to the anchor and I will do the same, promise me and we will make it! I will hold tight with my life and then the storm stops and then they were just drifting away from land and farther into the Pacific Ocean. Now it was days and then weeks, and no rescue at sight, but one morning a coast guard when by and thought the boat was empty and then they saw Kelly and Roger on the deck and barely alive and then the coast called a helicopter and then they were carried on to the copter and they were flew to a hospital in Los Angeles. About two hour later, Kelly woke up and looked around and said "where am I"? Kelly presses the button and the nurse came in and said "where is my friend"? Well he is in ICU. What wrong with him, well he infection some kind of virus and we cannot give him the right dose, because he will become a zombie, you are lying too me. No I am not. Just lies back, I don't want too tied you up, do you understand? Yes but I need to sees him, but he is really in bad shape he probably not to make it. Please I wants too sees him, then they heard a banged inside the halls and the nurse said I will be right back, and then it was silent and then Kelly heard sounds and voices and then Kelly got up from the bed and then peek out of the door and she saw that nurse were getting eaten up by the zombies and then Kelly was weak in her legs and thought to herself, I need to get out of here now!!! Slowly Kelly got dress and put on her shoes and pulls of the IV form her arm and then walks out in the hall they were busy eating the nurse brain and then thought she need to find Roger and get him out. But where do I find him and gets out this hospital and I feel that I am stranded in a hospital with thousand of zombies and I am also at home and then I just cannot talked too myself. Now what should do? I need to find my friend Roger and then we can leave him. "So where is that ICU? I don't know, it must be on this floor and I don't wants to stay that long on this place and get caught by night of the living dead. Grouse with body parts and splatter blood everywhere, i am getting sick and I really cannot walks I need a cane for now, went I get my strength and then I will have the energy, oh no! I don't know what to do, but run into the elevator and go on the next floor and find Roger. Kelly when inside the elevator and when on the seventh floor, and I was not sure I was going but I knew that I had to find a ways to stay alive and not gets caught by the zombies.

Am I going the right direction but I still sedative with the medicine and I feel like I should be sleeping but I am just walking in halls and I don't know if Roger is a zombie or dead, and I still keeps searching for him, I believe that I could end up, and then Kelly heard shooting and bombs and just looking out of the hospital that building were burning and the zombies kept on coming, and the military firing shot and the zombies were falling to the ground and then Kelly looked around and two zombies were about to velour her and Kelly ran and almost fell to the ground. But at moment, I thought I heard Roger yelling out and saying get me out, they will eat my brain, but hurried they are coming toward me, does anyone hear me? One of the zombie were about to grab Roger and Kelly just came behind the zombies and hit that zombie in back of the head and then came up to Roger and said, I need to looked into your eyes, so I will flash a light and I will sees if you are infection? Am I? So far I cannot see it.

ZOMBIES PART 2

I am not sure to let you go! But why, on your medical records says that you have the some blood that spread the virus and you will become a zombie, do I looked like I am going be one? At this point I don't know but I don't want to find out. Take a chance with me, I promise that I won't bite you, but you turn into a zombie, you will not care and you will only wants my brain, then you can shoot me, but now, I am fine, just trust me, you can tells how I act and how one become a zombie? But I am not sure what you saying? Just trust me and your intuition and you will not gets bitten and I will not have your "brain" for lunch or dinner, the doctor make a mistake with my blood, because mine is was always off, I don't understand, well when I was a child I had anemia, oh I sees that why they thought you had the virus, but we are wasting time talking and the zombies are gained up on us and we must hurried, yes I do agree with you! So let go and stop talking the possibility of me turning into a zombie.

About ten minutes later, the zombies were everywhere and where do we go and hide from them, I don't know but one thing, we need to leave immediately, yes and I am in back of you, said Kelly.

Roger was not really moving fast and Kelly said what wrong with you what did they give you? I think they gave me a antidote and it is making me tired, and I need to rest and Kelly said not now we need to move fast and out of this hospital and if we don't we will be trapped do you understand? Yes I do, but I will be behind you, Kelly, ok I will go and get to the "service Elevator" and I will wait until you comes too me, fine! Kelly got there and she called out too Roger and said they are in back of you and run too me now, but he was not able to do so and one of the zombie, got Roger and torn him into pieces and about hundred were coming toward me and I just

10

step into the elevator and when down and meanwhile, Roger was torn from limb to limb and his arms were torn off and the blood splatter and then one of the zombie, pull out the brain and then the rest took out the guts and liver and all of the inside, and meanwhile I was going to the garage and I didn't know if I was going too be safe, or I would run into zombies and unable to escape this nightmare. I got out of the elevator and then I looked around and so far I was alone and I walks up too a ford mustang and was about too open the door and then I saw them coming and I knew I had to find those key and drive away from here, so I search and search and they were coming closer and closer and at that moment I find the key and I started up the engine and I skidding out of the garage and when out of the garage and I saw so many of them zombies and I drove through them and I knew I couldn't stay in LA, I need to find a safe place for tonight and I was alone. But I knew there was no such place to go and I thought, probably if I when too the lab and I would go into the "secret room" and I would be safe, right now I was not thinking but I had no choice so, I decided to go there!

But every streets and I when down I saw Zombies, and I at this moment I didn't know, if I ran out of gas of the middle of the street and there were zombies, I would probably be "DEAD MEAT", and I sure I didn't wants that's ! So that day I drove like a crazy woman but I knew if I didn't, I would be dead and I am not going let it happened too me.

Now I am talking too myself and I don't have anyone too talked too and I don't know anything and the "special report" no one is on air and I feel that I am alone with zombies and I need to survive this and hope that some day that someone will rescue me and I will not be alone. Kelly drove for hours and hours and no one in sight but zombies, zombies, zombies, on every freaking streets and I am alone, and then Kelly tried to use her cell phone and no one answered, the sounds were getting louder and louder and they were getting closer too me and now I don't know what going too happened but I am not giving up., I think that I have a gun and few bullets to shoot a few zombies and then I will need to run for my life and not looking back… so I stops because of red light, and I didn't wants to break the law so I waited until the light change color and then I drive away and but the light was red and then the zombies were coming closer and then I speeding off and didn't looked back.

Now I was getting closer too the lab and I saw military standing around the building but I knew how to get in without them seeing me so I snuck out in the back through the basement and I got into the service elevator and press number 111 and then I push into the key and the code and I got into my office and make sure not too be seen and then I went on the internet and tried to find out the update about the virus but nothing, because I believe that it was classify, and top secret, now I knew that I was working with the government, to make weapon out of human and I was terrify, now I was thinking what have I done, if I knew I would never take this job and I would not make the antidote that were made you a zombies, Kelly was angry and wanted to delete the files of the antidote and then the alarms when off and now I will be screws and they will know what I have done and now they will locked me up so, I need to find that secret room and hide out and I need to make some cameras and not too be seen, so Kelly walks through the halls of the lab that she use to work and the soldiers were coming to search for her and now I was really scare and I couldn't let them catch me, I would end up dead. At last I reach the room and I will be safe and I need to make sure that I have the antidote and some water and not gets infection and put in the password and then, I can relax, and then Kelly locked herself in the room and the soldiers were roaming the hallway and searching for me and then they left but I still stay there and also I had a laptop computer into the room and I knew I needed to keeps them on track and I would not be caught or killed by military or the zombies. I knew that they were found me but I still working on how to solve the virus and how to escape this nightmarish dream that was possible to forget, but at the same time thinking that you were be alive tomorrow, and not shot by the solider or by the zombies.

I knew that I was trapped in the "secret room" I know that they will break the code and I will have no place to run, the worst scenario is getting killed. But the most fear that I have that Zombies breaking in and getting me and I don't wants that's! For now I will be quiet and hope to god that no one found me! But now I hear sound in the hallways and they are coming near and I need to hide and make sure that they don't see me! So where do I hide, then I just remember that there was a secret passage on the bottom floor that open with a remote and there would leave me to the bottom floor and then I got to the garage and I find a car and I drove away from there with a hospital gown, and I knew that I had to leave this instantly. I knew that I was not out of the woods, I still had to deal with the zombies and military, and I need to find a way out of that city. I got to the highway it was bar wire and the military they were coming from one side and then the zombies in the other side. I was in the middle and I didn't know which direction to go, so I decided to go on the back road and drive fast and not be seen. But I needed to found a house in the hills ands to hide out and not be seen by anyone at alls and I am fear of my life and I don't what will happened if I am caught by solider and bought to camp and maybe they will test me with the antidote and then they will make me be a Zombie" and I am not going to be a guinea pig for the government and how I sees things right now, they are not wining the battle but the zombies are winning and I am fear from both. So just keeps on driving until I find a safe place to crash and then I will barrack myself inside and get some electric fences against the zombies.

But I know that I am alone and I will not be alone to hook up a fence by myself and I think a way that I will be safe until the virus is gone, I will come out and walk into the yard and sit down and take a swim in the pool.

"Now I am searching for a place that I will be able to be safe and until it end". I don't know where to go and I don't know anything what happened with plague, and I just don't wants to get shot in the head, because I am not a zombie and I fighting until 2006 and now it is 2011 and so, and I am still alive but my family and friends perish from the virus and they are roaming the street of LA. I am driving unharmed and no one will save me, because I am alone, and I don't know why?

So many years I work in the lab but it was top secret, and I found out that they create weapon against there enemy and so how it backfire and now, there are thousand of zombies roaming the street and I am just about to run out of gas in front of this mansion and I guess I will be staying here for awhile and I will tried to put on the TV.

DARKNESS RISE!

At that moment before I got out of the car and drove inside and close the gate, and I looked around and it was clear and so I step inside and close the door and then I didn't put any lights on to have a attention that I was inside and then I used my flashlight and then I looked around and it was abandon and so I for a moment I sat down on the couch but I realized that I didn't closed the door behind me. Then I got up and then I walked to the door and then I checked near doors and windows and also put on the alarm, at this point I was not sure that it were work, but I felt secure.

" Then I find some candle and at this point I was not sure to lights them because once again I didn't want anyone too see me so I sat in the dark, I heard some creak and sound from the basement and I just when over there and locked it, and then I check my cell phone, put no signal.

Then I put on the TV to find out what was going on, and it was just that signal with the warning and then I shut it off. I lie down on the couch and fell asleep. The next morning I woke up and the gate was open.

I peek through the hole and no one was there but I was very caution I knew someone was here, and then I heard a bang and boom sound in the basement and then I heard voices, saying "let us out"!!! Who are you and why are you in the basement? Well I am alone and my name is Dave

So Ted are in infection with the virus, no I got drunk with a friend and some how I ended up here and my friend just vanish and I cannot explains what happen. Well when was it about a week ago and I just woke up in this place and so I stay in the basement, I thought it was it was secure but I heard a lot of noises and then I got up and I looked around and I opens the door to the basement and then I took candle and started to walks downstairs, and then I looked and then I check each crack and crank in the basement and nothing and then I saw the door was opens and now I knew that I better to get the heck out of there now!!! Then I put the candle near the washer and then I saw a little child and like crying but at that moment, I didn't wants to touch the child, and I saw the fluids coming out of the mouth and now I knew I better runs and locked the door behind me and then, I put a chair against the door and then I looked around for a gun and then I when into the dining room and I saw a shelf and cabinet and then I open it and then I gun the 9mm and then and now I looked for bullets and once again, I felt safe in the house even though I knew that some zombies got into the basement door.

At this time I believe that I will be safe and protection and I locked myself in the house and no one can gets inside and so,, I was relief and then I can just sit back and wait for someone to rescue me and not shoot me in the head, but I didn't have many bullets but I have foods and waters for few month and this virus and I can go back to work. I just sit in the dark., and no new special report and then I don't know if the world will be but I am the only survive so far that I know of but I am just going to wait in this beautiful mansion. At night Kelly when into the main bedroom and cover the windows and lay back and fell asleep. The next morning I gets up and I looked around and I carry my weapon to make sure that I don't runs into zombies and if I do I will shoot them in the head and I know that I am safe right now, and about half hour later, and then check each door and but nothing and I was happy but I do dare not too step outside because I don't know if they are lurking from bushes, and I don't wants to be caught, and them having my brains, I refuse too lose the "battle". Now I seems like I am talking too myself and but I hope that you understand, that I am alone in the world with thousand of zombies. maybe by now million zombies and wanted my brain, and I don't what going to happened next but I am going to stay her and listens to the news and find out if I could find a place that I could be really safe... so Kelly step outside walks the ground and then about a minute later, I heard sound like trucks were coming through and then I ran inside and make sure that no one would sees me, and then when the trucks passed by and I thought it was clear but I was mistaking about that's the zombies, are coming!!! Now I ran and ran inside and closed the doors and they were coming on the streets and they were on the yard and I think that I was surrounded and they were moaning and saying "I want brains!!! Right now they were smelling me and I expose myself and now they wants to break in, and got more woods and I banged and banged until I was secure. I hid behind the couch and then I heard the window smash and now I knew that I have run to the car and drive away from here but I don't have diverse to get me out and now I feel trap and now probably be eaten by the powerful zombies. But I am not giving up... ands praying that there are mores survivors but I don't means the military, and the government that screw up with the plague that spread, and I am not going to let them find the military, in the first place they used it has a weapon and now it backfire and it there fault, but the antidotes that I worked on just didn't have a power effective, and I believe the last dose... maybe I should just test it out and I won't get the swine flu that was the endemic, well I am taking a chance, so I put the syringe into my arm and gave myself a shot. At that moment, I just fell to the floor of the house and it got dark, and I just lay there for hours and hours and I thought I was dead. I woke up and the room was dark and I thought I saw lights and so bright and then I slowly got up and I was shaking and off balance, so I walks to the couch. Then I sat down on the couch and then I was sitting, but I didn't feel the same, something was changing and my skin was pale and then I thought to myself what did I do? Am I stupid took the risk and now I would become a zombie, also it could backfire and then I passed out once again!!! About five hours later I woke up and seem like I had a bad dream and I was not sure, that I really took the antidote.

"Antidote Side Effective"

I just started to walks weird and my speech was not normal and now my appearance got change, you can says that someway I did turn into a zombie, and now I was really terrify, what have I done to myself and it could be a fatal mistake and I could gets shoot at this point. Drool was coming out of my mouth, and I knew that antidote was working but the side effective was the worst that I ever deal with and now I have wait until the antidote goes through my body and the side effective stops and I don't when but I am going too wait inside this house and make sure that I am not a target and gets shot in the head. I stay inside in a closure room without any windows and doors and I was holding on to the gun and if I needed too shoot I would, but I wouldn't wants to shoot an innocents, so I was very careful and also sleeping and off balance that day! That day I saw the "soldiers marching through this section of town and I saw zombies breaking into the house but I blocked myself and they have no ways of getting inside where I am secure, but I have no one to talked with so I am talking to myself and I hope that the crisis were be over. About half hour later, I fell asleep and outside there were shooting and zombies gained on to the soldiers and the battle just continue and I didn't sees who won the battle and I slept for day and days and then I woke up and I saw the house next door was burning and a lot of body parts, and I couldn't believe my eyes but I was lucky that they didn't crash through this house and bite me, I would not be able to shoot them because I would out of it.

I was tainted by the antidote, ands it was not getting better and I looked into the mirror. My face looks like a zombie, and now I was really worry am I dead, and I walks and eat brain, that moment it terrify me and I said no I am not going think that ways! " Time when on and on and

I checks my pulse and my heart and I was alive but I didn't recognized myself, I felt that I was going to be a zombie after that antidote, and I just sat and think and think that night and I fell asleep and I woke up and I did feel okay!

But then I was walking I didn't feel that I was strong, and then I looked out of the window and they stood and were looking inside and now I knew that I couldn't stay here for long, and I said well I will go into the car and drive off and so someplace else and not to be caught by the zombies and the military, they were tested me…no ways! I refused, and I am not going to be a lab rat for them, I did works in a lab and I made this antidote and now, I am getting the side effective, I am screws.

Well, I am going drinks a lot water and I will flush it out and then I will be fine, I thought too myself and I thought what a ass I was about taking the antidote, time when by and I was still alone and getting worry and paranoid about getting killed and then, I was fine, and then I was going to leave this place and head south. I was confuse and mix up after taking the antidote, but now my head is clear and I feel the crisis are over and now I can just think what I am going to do next and I also need to get some gas for the car and I also need to shoot a hundred zombies out of my window, so I will be a bit busy and I will get the hell out off from this hell hole and get someplace hot and I can just rest in the sun and not worry about the zombies. now I need to get my gun ready and aim and shoot, but I am a bit dizzy and foggy but I will be able to make it too the car and drive away, I hope so, and I will not have no one to save me. But I am going to think positive, but I do missed my friends Tina and Roger and when I needed a distracted, they helped me out and then when they got both of them and now I am lost, and I don't know what to do with myself,, well one thing that I am not infection and the side effective are going and now I just need to leave this luxury mansion and hit the road and not been seen by military and the zombies and I am surviving the endemic, and the antidote, and I will survive the rest, about a minute later, I heard sound and I was about too leaves but tanks and trucks were coming through and now I knew that I cannot notice and I need to get the hell out of here now, go I got into the car and then some zombies were coming my ways and then I stop and took off and drove and drove into the woods and I knew that it was not the right decision because I will be needing gas for the car and I knew I might the wrong choice but I didn't have no responsible for anyone but me. I stops and resting there and I walks for a while and I knew it was clear and no zombies around so I stay for one hour that day and then I got back into the car and drove off and when further into the woods, and I knew there a cottage near the lakes end of the road and I was going to stayed there for awhile. It was suppose be about a week and then it became to be month and then I decided stay longer, but then I thought, there I was safe, but then I saw them coming closer to the cottage and my doors were opens and then I started to break the wood and locked it tight and that they were not enter. I build the bar wires, and electric wiring and then I knew that I would prevent coming into the yard, but if they broke down the fence I would be goner.

I thought to myself I am not safe even though they cannot get inside but I am still trap and they still wants my brains and so I just have too shoot them and when I run of bullets I will just drive off into a different directions.

That was the plan but then, I heard from the "zombies we wants brains" it was so close, that I thought I was it was all in my mind but it was not, the alarms when off and they were coming to the cottage and now I had to get ready too aim and shoot and not to waste a bullets.

I was outnumbered by the zombies and then I heard sound and then I saw a man with long blonde hair in a ponytail and you can called him, Brian and he called out and said " can I help you"? And I said yes! Then he drove too me and had a machine gun and shot about twenty zombies and I ran too him and I left that place and I was not alone again!

I sat next him and he smell nice and he was such a sexy man and then he somehow gave me a kiss on my lips and not now later.

"You Save Me"

Kelly said to Brian, well you came the right time and you save me and the zombies were about inches away from me but I am just wandering why you have curtain in your car, well the sun bother my eyes and the curtain are my protection, oh I sees! Then he said, I won't hurt you, I don't understand? Sometime I am thirsty for blood, but why did you says that's! Kelly wanted to gets out the car when he said that's and Brian said, I promise I will protection you and I will not harm you and I am much stronger than the zombies, well what are you, I cannot says right now but I need to gets away from the sun and gets inside and we need to go now.

He was mysterious and sexy and I couldn't keeps my eyes off him and it was a long time that I was attractive to someone and I been alone so long, and I kept looking into his eyes and he was putting me under a spell. But he was getting very hungry at that moment he said I need to stops the car and walks into the woods and so would you close the door and I will be right back, and at that moment I didn't think of anything, until he came back with a bloody mouth and his fang and then now I knew he was a vampire, and now I wanted to leaves and he said, I will not hurt you. But at that moment I was terrify and said, why did rescue to be your meal? No! I just came by and you were damsel in stress and I just wanted to help you, I don't believe you, I don't want to be here, and then he said go and you will be eaten by those zombies. And I will not be able to save you, well I am willing to take my chances and I never deal with vampire. Well, Brian when we reach the next town, I will just go, no you cannot go, because the virus spread and there is no safe location too be.

I am trying to believe you but I just don't, and then he looked into her eyes and then she said, come to me, and he kissed her lips and then they make love in the car and then she said "you put a spell on me" and once again she kissed his lips and then she said I was wrong about you, and the sun was coming out and he said, "I wants you do the driving" ok I will!

But where are we going? Well we are headed out of LA and then we are heading too Detroit Michigan, and we will stick out the virus there and we will be safe, because the virus didn't spread that quick there and the air is cold and so, my family is there, I don't understand? Well your vampire family? Yes but they do not bite human for blood and they drink pig blood, and I guarantee that you will not become a vampire. So Kelly kept on driving, and knocks down about one hundred of zombies, and Kelly was relaxed, and then they came to the blockade and now what? How do I get around this obstacle? So that moment she woke up, Brian, and said how do get to the other side. "Brian got out of the car and removes the fence and gate and then he wave and Kelly drove the car and then Brian got back inside and that was easy but why was it closed? Then they saw the zombies, coming closer and closer what why we comes here? We need to cross that bridge and I didn't know that they were here.

Went I was going to LA this place was non zombies, and now it is swamped. But it will be not be difficult to get out of here and we are about one mile from the bridge that crosses to Seattle, and then heading north and then southwest and then to Michigan, and then we will be safe. But I am not sure at this moment but I will help you out and I will killed those zombies, and I will break them into pieces and I don't wants to hears that, well you do almost like the zombies, but don't put into the same level, we are very intelligence and we will survive the this ordeal if I am the last vampire standing, well probably you will.

But please don't says that's, my peers were be very upset too get killed, alls my friends were killed and I am the only alive that I know. Well I don't wants to talked about miserable and pain and I just wants to make it and move on and be happy and in love, you will Kelly, and I would like to have children some day, you will! Then he stare into her eyes and some of my friends, are not that friendly has I am, they might wants some of your blood but I will not let them gets you, now you tells me when we are half ways there and my choice of place would been, New York, but I agree to go with you and now, I will not change my mind and so, Brian I will stick with you and I will be careful and not be off guard with your vampires friends, and I need to tells you after the earthquake, you must know that there are "DEMONS", what? Well there are "zombies, Vampire, Demons,,, that I need to be careful, yes, and demons will tried to convince you that we are the bad guys but they will tried to gets your soul., no I don't wants to hears that, I have enough problem with the zombies and now with the vampires and demons, yep! I don't like it and it is not like it was before, and Brian said we were around but never seen, oh I sees. Well you were hiding from the world? I don't wants to talked about it so let keeps driving from this zone and into a better place, I don't understand, and I am the only human around I think, well you could be wrong, maybe there are more, well I was fighting this battle since 2006 and now it is 2011 and still didn't lose the battle but there were close called. I know what you mean lost a few of vampires, because they are zombies and demon say start between I signed a agree of peace, and then they just left and then this happened and it became chaos and no control. Brain was then than here our destiny Kelly didn't know if she likes being this situation with Vampires. About one hour later they arrive to Michigan, and they were swamped by Zombies and then Brian said I see my vampires torn into tiny pieces and we need to leave this place immediately, but why we just got here! But looks, out of windows and you sees bloods and body parts and zombies coming toward us, yes, I will turned the car around and I also shoot those zombies, but you don't have enough bullets, just go! Okay, I will!

MAYHEM AND DEATH PART 2

Looked around they are coming closer and one zombies grab the back of the car and Kelly tried to push him off and but no luck yet! More speed Kelly, I am, not worry, we will be fine, I know how to gets around and get the hell out of this place, fine! But Kelly was getting closer to Brian, she felt some kind of attractive too him, even though he is a vampire, and Kelly knew that she was changing and Kelly didn't feel the same has before and she saw her appearance was changing since the antidote and now she knew that she will probably change into a zombie. Meanwhile zombies were coming closer and closer and it was more difficult to kill those zombies, they were much stronger than the other ones.

But Kelly knew that she had to tell Brian to drop her off, about two miles and she were be alone and he said "I don't understand what you saying, because I don't wants to hurt you" you won't, how do you know that's, I just know, well I took the antidote and it is causing me problem, but what kind, what? I don't understand, well, I might become a zombie, no it is your mind playing tricks, but you look the same, take my word, Kelly. Brain said that we are not too far to my friends so we can hide out there, but the population of zombies is growing and no one is not out there killing them, where are the military and the forces, well they are probably dead, and maybe zombies, I don't like too hears that Brian, but I am glad that I am not alone, and I am glad that you came along, well you that I am the undead, and I am a vampire, yes I do and I do feel safe with you, I am glad, so am I, and once again he kissed her lips and then hold her tight. Well, I think it time to leave this place but I need to killed that "ZOMBIE" to step out of the car and kill that zombie, please to be careful , I will and I am much stronger than that zombie, yes you are not tell the

23

zombie grab you, he won't! Kelly looked out of the window and saw Brian get close to the zombie, and then Brian was about to get bite and Kelly ran out of the car and then Kelly shot the zombie in the head and Brian said I was fine I was going to killed that zombie, and you came to the rescue and so now we can go now, good, and then they both got into the car and they saw about one hundred came out the alley and toward us and us and we speed out of there and got into a main street and I thought we would be clear from zombies but we were not more body parts and blood stains and zombies with blood dripping from there mouth and some zombies with body part in there hands and then some eating guts and livers and then, some just go terrible to looked at, but they seen us when we got into that area, and Brian said I took a wrong turn and I need to take an other turn, well do it what are you waiting for? Okay! I will be able to do and just sit tight and then we will be very careful and then we will reach my friends and then we will be in "safe haven" I hope so, and then Kelly started to vomit and said what wrong with you, I told that I have a bad effective from the antidote and I am not that well, that is not good and we are so close to my friends and now you are not well, they will wants to shoot you, but maybe, I will put into quarantine and they will be safe, well you do think that I am changing into a zombie, not exactly, but just being caution, well what do you says about that's! We will be there in five minute and so this the plan, went says get out the car, you do and follow me, got it! Good, and make sure that they don't grab you. Don't worry they won't and I will be fine and we need to make a diversion and then we will be able, too sees your friends, and then we can just leaves and go to a different place, but my friends will refuse to leaves this place this place is like a sanctuary, but I believe it hell, and there will be no end of the virus, because it is the "swine Flu" and Brian said well I am vampire and I won't get the virus but I could end up, if hundred of zombies grabbed me and I will not be dead, but you are? Well, yes but I do have the intelligence and not like a monsters, my kind been killed by those low class zombies and they torn up a part, pieces by pieces, I know my friends are also shredding to pieces and guts coming out and liver and heart, and kidney, are being eaten by the zombies, and looked out on the street, there are "zombies" coming this ways, and then Brain friend came out and said, I will fight them with my fist, and I will gets them in the neck, I wouldn't do that'! But why not, because you get infection and you will died, and even worst you will become a zombies. No, I will not take my word! Why not, I was just trying too help you, well Kelly, I know how to killed a zombies and I don't need your advice, all right!

"But Kelly couldn't believe what she was seeing on the street and so many deaths and so, so many zombies and the virus spread and the endemic, did not end and the vampires were getting restless and they knew that they had have a battle between Vampire and Zombie, because the blood supplies was getting tainted by the zombies and vampire were dying from lack of blood, and Kelly thought they were going to help her to help the human race but they were hungry like the zombies, but they were after the blood, and more the peoples got infection, the vampire could drink the blood, it were make the vampires very sick and vomited and zombies, were winning the battle, and the military were loss each time, because of zombies coming in packs, and the military had less and less soldiers and they out of the city and hid the bunker.

Meanwhile, there was a new President that didn't know the protocol and the President did want to send out the nuclear bomb but the zombies stomp into the secure building and there were slaughter and mayhem and pieces of human flesh and blood on the floors.

But President and his wife hid in the secret room, where the first president got slaughter and killed my zombie, and he told his wife, that to be quiet.

BATTLE ZOMBIES AND VAMPIRES!!!

Brian said to Kelly, well I need to get my forces and march outside and beat those zombies, and you are going to leave me alone inside, well you can join us, but I had a enough of them, and they are not going to win, well you only have five vampires and yourself, I think, I will help you, I think that you should stay inside and closed the door behind us, but I can use my gun and shoot them in the head, but there are hundred and you don't have so many bullets that is true, but stops talking, and I will! Kelly said well I will wait for you, and I will shut the door tight and don't let any zombies inside, I won't! the five zombies walks outside and the whole bunch of zombies came toward Brian, Lou, and Bobby and Roberta, and Jill, and Jill was the first too go and Roberta said, I am not that powerful so I will go inside and Brian said no, you are staying until we finished them up.

Roberta, said fine, I shall stay and hope that I won't be slaughter like a pig and chew up and be in pieces, come on start thinking positive and you will be fine, I trust you, and they kept on fighting and then suddenly Roberta fell down and about ten zombies chew her up and torn her into pieces, and blood stains everywhere! So far Lou, and Bobby and Brian were defeated those zombies and then, Lou was surprise and then two zombies grabbed him and down he was on the ground with his gut pull out and dripping blood and drool from the zombies, and eating body parts, of the vampire, and Kelly was about to opens the door and then she saw a few zombies near the door and then shut the door tight.

Kelly looks through the window and Brian was still fighting and she started to hears, we wants brains, no! they were standing next too the door and Kelly said, I am trapped once again, if I step out I will be " Dead

Meats" , and I will not allow it, Kelly thought to herself., no! I need to survive this.

Then Kelly looked into the mirror and once again her face looked like a zombie, no it cannot be happening to me! It is a nightmare, stops!

Kelly looked again and she was relief that she was just freaking out for nothing! Then I looked out of the window, and I knew that it was not too long too wait for them to comes inside and I just was just losing my patience and I just didn't wants stay inside the house but I just listens to what Brian said and he was the one that bought me here and he did give me good advice., well but then she saw Bobby fell down and then a few zombies got him and he was torn into tiny pieces and blood splatter in the street and I said so how the zombies are powerful and I think how long they became zombies and the immune system didn't consume the energy of speed, I need to tell Brian too be caution and about there strength and energy and how to slow them down, and I don't have the antidote, and I only I can do only shoot them in the head.

I don't wants to lose, my friend Brian, but I know that he will beat those terrible zombies, and help to get the world has before the endemic, and the virus, and now I need to run out and fight with Brian and get rid of the zombies, now, then I heard a bang at the door and I looked and it was about twenty zombies,, so I will wait for Brian too come back. I waited and waited and it was getting later and later and then I knew that the sun was coming soon and I needed to warns, Brain was the last standing and I called out and said, just leave that zombie and get inside, right now, before the sun, will burn you, don't worry, just go inside and I will be there in a moment, fine! The sun was coming in very quickly and Kelly decided to run out of the house with a blanket to Brian, to save him from the zombies and at that moment, two zombies wanted to bite Kelly but then Brian, bite him in his throat and then the zombie fell to the ground and then the two zombie was more progress and strong and now, Brian had a problem of killing him and then Kelly somehow got a pipe and hit the zombie in the head and the second zombie fell and dies and then they both walks inside and close the door and then Brian yelled at Kelly, I told you too stays inside and you didn't listens and we both could end up dead, do you understand what I am saying? Yes but you almost killed if I didn't comes out and save you, do you understand what I am saying, to Brian, and Kelly sat down on the sofa and Brian got closer and wanted to kissed her and Kelly said no, I am not in the mood, just leaves me alone, what wrong? Nothing, I just want too be left alone, and Brain said fine!

·

Kelly sat in the dark and Brian when side his coffin, and lay down and slept until when night came, he came out of his coffin and Kelly was fast asleep and he walks outside and lock the door behind him and walks for miles and he walks into alley and he was surprise by zombies and he thought he were end up dead, but he was powerful and killed them, and then Brian was looking for blood and the only blood Brian got was Zombies blood, every times that Brain drank the blood, he got very sick and vomited every time, and then Kelly woke up and then heard him and she said you when hunting and you only drank zombies blood and now you are sick and Brian said, I don't wants talked about it, fine, but you can some of mind, no I might drain you out and you will dies, no you won't I will stops you! I will be so strong and desire to drink your "blood" and I will have no controlling and I am so hungry, that I just drain you dry, okay!

So, you cannot have my blood, and you cannot bite a zombies, so you will dies, but we need to get too a hospital, where there is blood and not use tainted blood, and you will lives, you are right but where is a area hospital? About I think about a mile away! but we will first have go through the zombies, so we need to get into your car and I will cover you with the blanket and then we just can leave, but you don't know Michigan, but you are might be right, where we are going? I hope so; I don't want to end up dead neither. I know. Yes I know what you mean, and we will make it, I know, you are strong, Kelly, thanks! But we are not safe and the zombies will follows us and tried to get inside the car.

VAMPIRE'S TERRITORY

Meanwhile Kelly and Brian were in the car and driving to the hospital to find blood for Brian, and not tainted bloods, that he was draining from zombies and getting very sick, and Kelly said I also need to find food and water, because I feel, light headed, and I am losing my energy to go on! Soon we will be at the hospital and we will check out the blood banks, but we do have a slight of a problem. What is it? zombies are blocking the door to the hospital, well I will get out of the car and killed a few, well I will comes out and helped you, Brian, now they are hearing from the zombies, we wants brains, brains, brains, I think we should drive away from here, but why, my food supplies is inside and I am going too find it, okay! Yes I just don't wants to be alone in the car and I do want to help you, I just feel that I am not helpless, said Kelly too Brian, but you are not and I will do fine without you. Brian left the car and Kelly locked the door and had her gun ready to shoot, but Brian got inside and search the lab with the blood bank and Kelly sat in the car and then she was surround by fifty zombies and mores were coming and now Kelly was scare and Brian was in the hallway near the "blood bank" and heard sound of moaning and creaking sound of the floor, and then he saw about ten zombies coming toward him and he got them in the neck and Brian got sick and fell to the ground and at that moment he thought he was going to dies, but then Brian got strength and bitten those zombies and spite out the blood and walks toward the lab and find the blood that he needed and before he took it, Brian taste it and it was good and he took it and walks out and saw the zombies around the car and dropped the blood and started to fight with the zombies, and then the military came and they started to shoot in the head and Brian almost got hit and then got inside the car and drove away without the blood, and Kelly said well once again, you will starve, no I won't! I have two bags in my pocket. Will that we enough for now, yes but don't worry about it, I won't! Fine! I am just trying to be a friend, well you are and you know that I am vampire, and it doesn't bother you, nope! Why not? Because looks out there, I know they are zombies and you a vampire and I believe I have a better chance with you and not with them, but when hungry strike, than you have too be careful with me, fine! But you don't even have a cross to protection yourself from me,, well I don't need it because I would stake you and you were be dead, but if you didn't sees me coming than you were be dead, so don't scare me, I have a lot on my mind right now., fine!

We need to figure out to get out of here, we will don't worry! Even though there are thousand of zombies out there, we will make it.

I will take you too a safe location and I will leave you, but I don't wants to be alone, but you will be safer. Fine, but I don't like being alone, with you I feel safe with you, well I am the undead, I know, but your need to blood and I am your food supply, that is true, but I do get other source of blood that I would not kills you, or other human. I am glad too hear about that's! Then Kelly looks at Brian and Brian looks at Kelly and then once again he kissed her lips and then they make love in the backseat of the car and then Kelly said we have too stops because they are coming and I don't wants to be dead meat for the zombies, I don't wants that neither, and they stops and then Brian started up the car and then he said looked someone head they have in there hands, those zombies are vicious and hungry and they just wants to eat brains, that is true, and I don't want to be there meal, and let go now!!! They were about half miles of Michigan and Kelly said that is a relief and maybe will find some living peoples around and then they heard tank and jeeps and they were coming into town and Kelly said find a alley and we just have to hide out and Brian does not question her and just drove in and hid until they drove away and then they got back into the road uptown and they looks around and Kelly said, well I just wants to looks around and then Brian said don't be a target out there and I won't! about a minute later, Kelly when inside a restaurant and I sat down at the table and then Brian came in and you must be kidding, that you are sitting here and think that you will be serve, no I just want to rest and he said we should barrack this place, and we will stay here for the night, fine, so I will bring the blood inside and Kelly was sitting at the table and thought it was Brian but it was a old lady and things were coming out of her mouth and then she called out to Brian, at that moment I didn't have the weapon to kill that zombie, at that moment I thought I would end up dead and then Brian when up to that lady and bite her and pull out her brain and she fell to the ground, and blood was dripping out and splatter the restaurant and Kelly, said we are fine, I think.

Don't worry, we can stay here and then leave in the morning, well I have a carving for pizza. Well do you see any place like that opens now? No but I would like to tried Jet Pizza sometime when things get back too normal, that is true, so Kelly, do you think that we secure? Yes we are secure and we are able to stays a few nights and then leaves at night of course, yes and I am fine with that's! then Kelly got ready for bed and Brian was ready to drank his blood and now he wanted more bloods, and he someone snuck out and search for a victim and he knew that he would drinks anymore of zombies bloods, and he was searching and then he find a teenager girl, and he name was Melody and he came up to her and looked into her eyes and bite her neck and drank her blood and then Melody fell to the ground and about ten minutes she became a vampire, and then he said, you need to comes with me, and you, who are you? Not now, you will not be safe her alone, oh you means the zombies, Yes! Let me introduce myself, my name is Brian and I am your maker, what is that? I am the one that made you a vampire; well you should have asked me? Well I was a hungry and on the growling and you were there and I bite you and you became a vampire, and about ten minutes later, Kelly said who is she? Well she is Melody and now she is my friend, well you have bitten her and she became a vampire, how could you? Well I was hungry and I didn't want her to die. But she is dead and now she is a vampire, I guess I cannot trust you; you can take my word, okay! Kelly was furious with Brian and she didn't wants to speak with him at that moment but she was silent with him and just chat with Melody and Melody said she was lost and no one to help her and then she got bitten by Brian and now, Melody said I have the hungry for blood and I won't bite you, thanks that is a relief, well I was surprise and off guard and I been chase by zombies and then Brian came to the rescue and he bite and now I am the undead, now I am vampire and I have no lives and soul, and then now I cannot go back to my family and now I just have to feast on blood and once I been a vegan, and now I blood sucker vampire, and the chaos what going out there I could been infection the virus, but it just turned out to be vampire, and it just happened to quick and I don't blame, Brian, I think that he save me, you being undead and thirsty for blood, I don't think so, he just was selfish about himself and you just were in the wrong place, well, I could been torn into pieces and now, I am just intelligence vampire with strong powers, and I can destroy those flesh eating brains zombies and send them to hell, where they belong, well you are a bit like a chip on your shoulder,, those zombies killed my family and I do wants too killed them but you a bit harsh, are you? Yes but I will killed them and I will kills them with a gun and shoot them in the head.

"Kelly called out to Brian and said why did you killed that innocent person and make her into a vampire"? well I was alone and you were a strong person and I didn't want you, so I find Melody and she will be my mate and we will travels and we will be leaving you and you will have to find our living persons on your own, I might find out someone out there, so after the sun goes down, Melody and I will be going and you are abandon me and what will I do alone? Well, you survive alone and you will be fine. All right! I am sure I will be, about midnight, Melody and Brian; walks out of the restaurant and left Kelly, Kelly called out and said 'how will I get out here"? You will figure out how, I will? They both drove off and Kelly was alone, I locked up the door and I sat in the corner and then I heard knock, and banged, and broke down the door, "zombies are getting inside and now I need to get out. Kelly ran out and looks for a car but they would smash and now I need to walk out of "Grand Rapid, Michigan, and I walk, and walks and I got end of road out of city, and I was safe again!

Kelly thought to me why I am in hell and it started with "swine flu".

No, it was flu shots and that started the virus, and I need to find the vaccination, and need to go there, destroy it, then the infection will be extremely danger and spreading, very rapidly will it end, I don't think so.

How will I stop it, but I cannot do alone, I need help me!

"ZOMBIES WORLD"

I am daze and alone in the "world" and no one there only zombies and no one else, even the vampires left and the werewolves and demons, and but were the living? But I am a sole survive and I am still alive and no one will save me but I am not going to become a zombie, I refuse.

But thousand and thousand were following me and I just kept walking and trying to gets ways. But they would get closer and ran and they follow me, and I ran into a building, and they were inside and they would inside and now I didn't know how, to gets out of here. But where and it is not clear and it is block by zombies and why did I go inside here am I a idiot, no but I thought it were be safe but I am not just being surrounded by zombies and now trapped and no one will save me, will they, find me and I will be home with my family and I am living with zombies world.

But I never been this situation since the time in lab went everyone became a zombies and somehow I was lucky, I think because they took the "flu shot" swine, and I refuse too take it and then rest infection.

They started too comes to me and try to get my brain and I somehow got out there with my life and I knew that the world was infection but I didn't know how many peoples were, but states that I when too there were zombies, from adults to children, and baby that I just killed right away! Now I knew that I needed to find someone to help me too killed those zombies or find a cure, but some were too gone to fix so they needed to be destroy and I didn't have the weapons, and I was trapped inside this malls that I shouldn't have gone, but I was not thinking but not I need to find a way out and be safe and not be seen, by the zombies.

"Well I needed a diverse to get out of the mall and go back into the streets where thousand and thousand zombies in the street, and neither

I stay inside and get caught or I take a chance and run for my life and find a car and leave this city of zombies. but I knew I were get the same situation where ever I when, but I didn't want to be "dead meat" and I didn't become the undead, that I would shoot myself instantly. Wait a minute, I am not giving up my life and I know that I will make it and it will be fine but I need to find a low population of zombies and not like a million of them at once, so I think that I should go to the countryside and It will be easier to deal with but first I need a plan to get out of this nightmare that I put myself in. well I don't know but I am talking to myself and I think, someone out there will hears me and will be save my a hero and my new love,. Now I am fantasy, that my prince charming would comes and rescue me and take me away from this terrible place., and the zombies were be gone, and the world were be back to normal., but that is impossible dream, since 2006 and it five years later and it still going on and I don't have knowledge to stops it and it someway it was my fault because I invention the antidote that went wrong and now, the world is with zombies in it, and I am alone and hungry and thirsty and I don't have the strength to beat them, and I sure don't wants to be one, so I don't have a solution, but one to get the hell out of here,, and hearing, I wants brains, and brains, now I knew that I need to go now and no one will stops me and even the living dead,, that spread very quickly and now I just thought what were my chances just walking out of there and walks in the middle of the zombies, would they know that I was not but I was not sure what to do, well I know that I couldn't stay here, so now I need to be brave and walks out and take my chancing,, and then I saw a military tank coming at that moment was about to step out and then they surround the tank and they were shooting those zombies and then I thought if I went out now, I probably were get killed and so I just hid in the corner and waited until the "battle" was over and I said to myself, I am going out and I don't care what happened to me, and I cannot stay here! Also I was been follows, by zombies, and at that moment I ran for my life and I didn't looks back and the tank got hit and the zombies got into tank and killed alls the "soldiers" and this place was not for me so I just kept on walking and didn't looked back and now I am out of Michigan and going toward Chicago,, and I don't know if that place will be better or not but I am going to make it alive and not be infection by the zombies, I am not going to lose the battle of survive, and will make.

"But I was getting tired and I don't have the energy to move on and so I needed to stay the night and think what my plans, so I don't what I will do, but I will not be caught by the government that don't know what going on or they are not around more, and there is not martial law. Just seems like the zombies are controlling the world these days. I am one living human and I cannot stops alone and I don't have nuclear weapons and I don't have access to that kind of power and I don't know if I am going to make it this time, but I am trying to be positive and survive this ordeal, and everyone that I know they are neither dead or a zombies and but I don't like the scenario that I am in this situation, but I need to find a TV or radio and hear a update about the virus, and there must be a place that I can live without zombies, but where is that place? So I decided to go inside the city hall of Chicago and it seems clear and I check around and I blocked the doors and windows and I didn't sees any zombies and I thought maybe Chicago was the place to be at this moment. That what I thought, and I just sat there and I prayed every night I would not died a hand, of the zombie, and not to get infection, because I felt sometime that I was going to become a zombie, but you should remember, that I took the antidote and I think that I was safe but time will tell, sometime it infection peoples, not the same ways, and I was not sure why I took it, but I did and it probably save me but not sure that I could become the living dead myself and I were not even know. But now I might sound paranoid but I try not to think that ways.

FLU SHOT WENT WRONG!

Time when by and I was still inside the city hall and no one around and I was getting really hungry and like I was going crazy and I was alone and I didn't have no one to talked too, so I decided to go to the mayor office to check it out and I didn't think that I was going to run into zombies.

That didn't cross my mind and then I knew that it was a mistake. Seeing bodies parts and splatter bloods and zombies with half of the jaws sticking out and drool coming out there mouth and hearing, brains, and I was on the top floor and I was seeing what was happening outside and I was really terrify and I thought myself, am I really safe up here? At this point I didn't know but it was really gruesome out there and I didn't wanted to a static, so kept myself inside and I know I couldn't stay there forever, I knew that had to go out into the world, and unknown that was happening.

But, I could been the one started it because the meat was tainted with bacteria and it make peoples sick and the lettuce and tomatoes, and water and the especially the "FLU SHOT", for the swine flu, that affective a whole bunch of immune person that the virus spread,, and now I am seeing the results, that peoples are dying and becoming "Zombies".

I cannot look outside, it is so terrible to bear, and I am the only one alive, and I have too deal with this mayhem and death that is unfair.

Once again, I am speaking to myself and no one is hearing me but I just heard a sound in the hallway and I don't like it, I think that they came here and I am scare, and I don't have weapon and I will be dooms, I will not jump out of the window, I will just steps out and take my chances, and I will survive this, and I will think positive about this situation and I will not lose it, do you understand? I was about to open the door and then I looked over and I saw a radio and wander if there any update, about virus, and but they were still trying to get inside and I put the desk next to the door and a chair and then I thought well, maybe the phone will work and I will called someone to rescue me, and I did and I got someone on the line and I thought at first it was a zombie, I was afraid to speak and told her where I was, if I was wrong, they were find me and then I were be dead meat, and I hesitate what was saying and the lady on the phone said go to the roof on top of the city hall and a helicopter will pick you up in five minutes, and I said I was in the mayor office and I was barrack and I was afraid to step out, but the lady said if you wants to be rescue, come out on the roof now!! So I remove the desk and chair and unlock the door and I peek through the hole and it was clear, so I ran so fast to the steps to the upstairs and I open the roof door and there were two zombies feeding on the mayor of Chicago, at that moment, the helicopter arrives and I stood there being patience and I knew I would be caught but the helicopter landed and I ran too it and got inside and then the zombies notice me and then the helicopter left the roof and I was safe and I asked where are going? At first he didn't answered, then he said, we are going to Detroit Michigan, but why, that is the clear zone, and then he introduce himself, and said his name was Jeff, and nice to meet you, same her and you are my first rescue in 30 days, well there are no other one? So far no! but I need to tells you we are not flying by helicopter but we will be going to the airport and take a private jet, so we will have to go through the terminal and we might run into zombies, yes I know and this is not my first time, mission to rescue a beautiful lady like you, well I was in this situation since 2006 and still dealing with it, that is a long times.

But we have the situation handle and you can just rest at the army base and you will be secure from the zombies, well where are you going well I am going to killed those zombies and I wants to come along with you, even though you rescue me and I am able to shoot and killed some zombies, but Kelly you are not in the military and you just an ordinary person and you need to takes my order and you too stay here, well I don't wants to stay here and I wants to fight and killed those zombies, do you understand they killed many of my friends and my family and it alls cause by the tainted meats and the flu shot for the "swine flu" and I think also with the antidote when wrong in the lab that I works on and I took a shot and I feel fine but I do have some of the symptoms of the virus and I think that we should contain you, miss, I will be fine.

Then Jeff called his captain and told him about Kelly and he said to locked her up immediately and Kelly you have betray me Jeff, thanks a lot, and now I am trapped and maybe will be tested like a rat lab. About one hour later, that Jeff told them they took me into a lab and it was really yucky and a lot of body's parts and bloods spreading and I said I am not infection and what are you doing? Well we were inform that you had the symptoms of the virus and so we need to test your blood, and Kelly, was rolls on the table and then like into a operation room and at that moment I needed to break out, because I saw skulls on the table and I was going to be dead and I didn't wants that and I didn't have the virus and I got to get through them that I am fine, but no one is listening too me, and I had to break those chains and get lose and get the hell out of there, and at that moment, they were coming in and then somehow I mange to get lose and then I got up from the table and then they tried to shoot me and I duck down and they missed me, and then I got up and I ran for my life and I being chase by ten soldiers, then I got into the jeep and I drove away and they follows and I got away and I hid in the woods and I knew, I were be safe for awhile and I knew neither the zombies were find me or the army, but I couldn't stick around too find out and I needed to get away from Chicago, now.

But I knew that I would have to use the back road to get out and if I use the highways, there were roadblock, so I didn't want to run into a solider again, and I don't need to be tested but to help with the cure.

Trapped Between Zombies And Soldiers

Soldiers were coming and zombies coming from a different directions and I was stuck in the middle and now, I needed to go underneath the bridge that no one were sees me, well I don't know, it I am spotted by the soldiers, I will shot at sight and then with zombies, I will be dead meat, but I need to take my chances and get the hell out, and find a safe location.

Meanwhile Jeff was flying over where I was standing and then he somehow landed and called me out, but that point I didn't trust him so I kept on running and he said I will help you, by turning me in? No I will get you out of Chicago and you will get court martial, no I will not why not Come on I will take you away, promise, yes my life depend on it.

But you be caught and then you be court martial and it will be my fault and you should just go and leaves alone, but they take you back to the lab and then they will cut you up and then they will killed you and I don't you to be dead, don't tell me that you fell in love with me and now you wants to save, yes, yes, yes to alls your questions, well, that is okay with me now! Okay I will come with you and I will be safe and I want you not too leave and stay with me, do you understand? Yes I do and I will not get caught and I will protection and we will get rid of the zombies, together. Soldiers coming from one side and the zombies from the others and Jeff said, well we don't have too worry and I will fly away and we will not be seen and then we will safe, I just know, well if we do get caught by the soldiers, and you will go to the prison and I will end up in the lab for testing and I don't like that scenario, I don't neither but we have no choice, and you are try so get into the copter and let leave this terrible place and then we can rest, I agree with you. About one minute later, the copter left the ground and Kelly and Jeff were relief and then the missiles were coming and Kelly said what going on here? I don't know think that we are threaten, well maybe we are, went we air what going on they will try to killed us to keep the secret quiet, I hope that we don't dies of the results off when just telling the truth, well we don't know how many peoples are alive and how many are zombies? That is true. But we should not worry about it now we are safe in the air and then we will land in a safe location and far away from Chicago and then we will be in Seattle, is not a good place well I don't know but we will be far way from soldiers and zombies I hope. Be positive I am but I am also worry about things that might happened if we gets the infection and I mean the virus, but Kelly you don't looks that good, seems like you changes, what? I don't understand, well seem, like you are a zombie, what? I just took the antidote and now I might be sick, well if become a zombie I will shoot you in your head and I don't wants to become a zombie, you won't me neither, I don't know what to says but hurried.

Are you sure? Yes I know I am the one that made the antidote and it seem it was the cure but there were some flaws in the antidote. I see and it does give everyone a different effective, oh and what is yours? Well mind is that started the virus and then the immune kick in. yes!

You might sees the symptoms occurs but they will not make me into a zombie, but some level, that I am not I do understand and you will not shoot me and I will be fine and I will helped you to shoot those zombies, and I will not comes up and bite your hand off and I will just be helping you, and says if I do turned into a zombie just shoot me into my head and burned me, I will Kelly, says if I got infection do the same for me, I will. Jeff ands Kelly headed to the coast of Seattle and Kelly said I have been here and we will not be safe, but they elimination the zombies and they are gone and are you sure? Yes I am and so Kelly and Jeff landed on top of the building and they got out of the helicopter and Kelly looked down and said we are still surrounded by them, no you are lying, no I am not!!! We need to escape now and we do not have no choice and we cannot stay here and time is ticking away and we will end being dead, so how do you know, I know how the "virus' works and so we better get the hell out of here immediately, do you hear me? Loud and clear, good and I am in back of you and we will leave this terrible place and so someplace that we can rest and not being dead meats that sound good to me.

Later that night, Jeff and Kelly got close and Kelly refuse to cuddle next Jeff so she just sat alone in the corner and then she felt chill and then Jeff asked what wrong Kelly, well I am fine, I still feel the side effective and it will take a while to get out of my system, me too. Are you sure that you will not turned into one of those zombies? Nope! It was happened by now and I am fine and I don't have the virus, good, and about you? Don't worry Kelly I am fine and I almost been bitten but I was not and that is the end of my story, well I don't wants to wake up one morning and you will tried to bite me and turned me into a zombie, how many times I am telling you and that I am not infection and I will not turned into a zombie.

I don't know, and where you were and what kind of shot you got from the special services, give me a clue, well I got the swine flu when the virus started to spread, so what did you get the PX doses or HH doses, I don't know and I don't know, so did you get sick and did you vomit and have sweating, no I didn't have those symptom, well I think that you got the right shot, and you seem fine so far, and you know the deal if I am infection and you killed me and you will do the same for me said Kelly.

Later that night, Kelly fell asleep and Jeff took a walks toward the city where the "zombies" roamed, and about half hour Jeff was trapped and he couldn't called out for help and meanwhile Kelly was sleeping and then she suddenly woke up and saw them standing right next too her.

Kelly didn't know what to do but she got up in a hurried and she looked around and called out for Jeff but he didn't answered her and now Kelly had a fear in her eyes and she was worry this time that she probably were dies, but then she looked and then pick up the gun and shot about ten zombies and she knew that she ran out and kept running and then Kelly saw that Jeff was surrounded and Kelly ran through the crowds and pull Jeff somehow and they both ran and when into the helicopter and flew away! Then Jeff said we forgot our supplies, well it is not my fault but yours that you wandering into that situation and then Kelly said I am sorry but I sometime cannot take it, I know I loss a lot of my friends so did I.

We cannot change it but we will try our best to do it but I don't know if we are going to make it, I know that we will make it and we will not die.

But don't promise something that you are not sure of, and I rather be ready to fight then died in the hands of the zombies.

I know what you are saying but I just cannot takes it too much and it is really stress me out and what do you think I am not stress out, of course you are and I do understand. What are we going to do now but I don't know at this point but we need to be silent and not to make a sound, yes I know the drill and you do not need to tell me over and over and I know that if they hears us they will break in and bite us and then we will be infection, yes, so we also cannot stay here and we need to move on and yes and not be notice, I think that I will gets pull the zombie inside and then we can spread the guts on us and then we will be able to travel and walks like a zombie, well if the soldiers sees us and then we can be shot in that case, that is true but we need to risk it, you are talking about my life.

Then they heard shooting and sounds of the zombies and a tank was coming through and then the tank stop and they looked at me and Kelly and they were about too shoot us and then we ran inside and then the tank got surrounded by zombies and they were shooting and fighting them off and Kelly said to Jeff this is the time to go and we cannot stay here do you understand, yes I do and I am ready to leave go need to go to the helicopter and fly away from here, yes but we will be seen by the soldiers and the zombies so we need to run for your life now, and no looking back, well don't forget the supplies and we will run and run until we get the helicopter and not gets shot in the meanwhile or bitten by a zombie, I totally agree with you, Kelly, stops talking and started running to me and we can escape this hell and we will be safe, you are probably right, I hope that you are. So am I! they reach the helicopter and but they had to deal with some of the zombies and Kelly was shooting them right in the head and didn't any and Jeff was not a great shooter and Kelly was getting a bit angry with him but she didn't yelled at him, because he knew how to fly the copter and Kelly got there first and then Jeff was about inches away and said, I am so exhaust and that I don't think that I can make it, comes on Jeff, we need to leave this place now! So he barely ran and almost fell to the ground and Kelly ran to him and said I will help you the rest of the way, and you need to show me how to fly.

NIGHT OF THE LIVING DEAD PART 2

Meanwhile in the helicopter,, that Jeff was weak and Kelly said show me how to fly and he said, I need to rest right now and then Kelly said we cannot rest now, they are coming toward us and the soldiers are getting slaughter, by the zombies and you need to get this helicopter into the air do you understand? I do but I don't have the strength. let me take over. Tell me what do and I will do it no! This is like suicides, I loss a lot of my friends and I don't know if I can go on, stop this and I didn't comes here to dies, I came to win this battle of zombies and you are like giving up on life, stop this ridicules, I cannot take it from anyone do you understand, but are like inches away from us and you still didn't start up the engine do you know you are risking your life and mind, then he turned the key and it were not start and that great! I must have flood the engine and it will take a minutes to start up and don't have that time they will get us.

About a minute later, the helicopter was in the air and they flew through the city and they saw mayhem and death all around them.

Kelly said to Jeff I don't wants to be here, I don't wants too sees this but you have no escape, I know then she got close to him and kissed him and Jeff said stop this. That night they got passion and Kelly said this could be our last night together and the zombies might get us, so we need to be close, I agree and that night they make love and the zombies were not too far way from them, and Jeff said we have only four bullets left and I think that we should use them on ourselves, Kelly said I am not giving up and I am not going dies,, looks in what situation that we are and you still wants to fight, yes I do and I am not a quitter, I am not neither but it does not looks good, and then Kelly got up and left him and she said I cannot be with you because you are too much of the negative, well you need to be positive, I am trying my best. Well I am not in the mood right now.

Kelly left the room and when into the storage and said this place looks secure and I think it will keeps us safe from the zombies for a while, if they break in and then what? We shoot out and we run for our lives and reach the car and drive away! So that is your plan for now. What is your plan I don't have one so we will stick to my plan and we will survive, you think? Yep, so far how I plan thing and they works out and I am not giving up on my life so you need to listen what I am saying. I am seems like you are and then you are not, what are you saying exactly well, never mind and then Kelly looked out of the windows and there were about thousand zombies standing near the window and seem like the window will be smash and Kelly was being quiet but also scare at that moment and try not to show it to Jeff, and she knew that one point there was no escape plan and they probably trapped, and then Jeff said well we need to run to the helicopter and get on and fly away again to an different destination and where are no zombies population, so where is that place? I don't know Kelly don't push me and I am very angry and worry that I AWOL from the military, and I am being hunted by them and zombies. You know what I mean. You are saying that when they catch you, you will end up behind bars, yes in a federal prison, and for running off with me, but my reason was that I save you from the military and not being tested and so I decided to break you out and get you out of here and also I didn't like to do there dirty works anymore. Okay I do understand why you left but now we need to find to be out of there radar and not to be caught by them.

So you must have a plan line up and you think will it work, I think it will and you will be safe from zombies and military and you we will able to escape from this place and so south and hide out until this is over and what do we do meanwhile well run for your life and then not too looked back,, I can do that's! We are heading to a new destination and we will be safe there you think? I think so and don't worry about it, I am worry about I survive the first time it happened in 2006 and now it is in 2011 and I don't if it the same but we need to be caution and careful where we go and not be spotted by neither the soldiers or the zombies and I don't wants to be dead meat, the soldiers first shoot and don't asked and then the zombies just bite you, so you are saying ours survival are slim, I hope not! But they are not good, I do understand but we cannot stand the middle of main street and you probably were get caught, yes so let move on and leave and find the safe haven and not be in the middle of the battle of the middle and soldiers, I agree and if you are caught you will be court martial and I will be send to a lab, that is true, to check if you are infection with the virus, I know that I am not and I did take blood test and it confirm that I am not, and they didn't believe me. I know you told this story and you dad was a general and he got slaughter in a battle and he didn't have chance to make it and that is true there were too many of the zombies. I don't wants to talked about my dad and it is too painful and the soldiers didn't help him out and they also got killed in the battle.

About five hundred were killed and counted and I don't like this and is there any latest news about the virus, so far no seem like it is the same.

Then Kelly put on the radio and there was a "special report" and said the virus is over and everyone can go home now! This it true, am I hearing that they killed the virus and no more zombies, that is good news said Jeff, yes it is so take me home to LA, well we will need to board a plane and fly home, so take me to the airport and I will buy a ticket and get home and sleep in my home again, that sound good, said Kelly, so I am going with you, yes you are and we will talked and get to know each others, I like that said Jeff, so Jeff and Kelly when into the helicopter and flew to the airport and bought a ticket to LA and seems like everything was normal.

About ten minute later they boarded the flight and they headed home to LA and Kelly and Jeff sat all the ways home and about one hour later they landed at LAX and they got out and there were no zombies, and soldiers and Jeff and Kelly walks out to the street and got a cab and heading on Hollywood BLVD and they were headed home and Kelly said do you wants to comes to my home and he nodded his head and said yes!

I don't know but will be safe, I think so, and I trust you Jeff.

Kelly follows Jeff and she thought she knew where he was going but at that moment she didn't know that they were be surrounded by the zombies and then Kelly said if I knew I would show you the ways out but you got us in this trapped, now what? I don't know, but what are we going to do, not to panic, I won't freak out if they grab your arms and try to eat our arm. Where do and we are in the open and we are going? Just run and run and find a place to hide and there is no place to hide and then Jeff find a car and then Kelly inside the car and drove but it was so close, that I thought I was a goner, but I am a survivor from the past and you place me into danger, how could you? I didn't think that we would going be trapped but we make it out and we are getting out here headed where no zombies around, there is no place like that's!

He drove and drove but his were shaking and nervous and he almost when in the ditch and Kelly said are you trying to killed us and you are doing a great job about it and don't be such a bitch, well I don't know how you survive this long and what are you being sarcasm, no but we need how to work together and get the hell of here, I do understand. Kelly said to Jeff, I been killing off the zombies since 2006 and you don't know how difficult it was and how I survive and my dad was a general and at the field the zombie got him and he was the one that save me from the quarantine and I almost got shot and killed and by soldiers and the zombies and now I am not going to let them win.

Looks they are everywhere and we have no place to go and they will catch up too you and we will be eaten and then we will roam the streets and we will become.,, never I rather died, what you are giving up, no but they are coming closer and closer to us and then they will gets ours brains and we will be torn apart and then we will not be alive.

I see what happening here and they will be coming and then Kelly said watched your back, I am. They are very close get your gun out and aim and fire, got it the drill, but it is a serious matter and we are the only two battle the zombies and we have no escape but we will killed those zombies and who ever created them,, they shoot be shot and a lot of innocent peoples are getting killed and the night of the living is a bad nightmare, yes it is and I am, and Jeff said we will need more weapons and bullets and not sure that we will killed them alls but we will tried and then we will leave this place and go toward the east and I think they don't have the epidemic and I think first we need to deal with this ordeal and then we can find a place to sleep and eat and find a car for transported and we will be better and safe and so looked how many of them and we have no way of stopping them, no kidding, said Kelly..

TIME RUNNING OUT

When I tell you too run you run and I will be in back of you, I promise you Kelly and I never lies, I don't know that but I will trust you and I will go to the edge of town and find a car and we will be able to escape and no turning back , fine and you need to be strong, Kelly and you cannot get weak, I fought a lot of fight and I didn't lose, and this time, I won't neither so Kelly ran out of the street and she was surprise and that she was surrounded and then Kelly couldn't get out of there and what do I do, to Jeff, get out of there I cannot I am trapped and no your not bend over and cross over and get to the other side of the sidewalk and walks to that black car and sees if there are keys in the car, if there not but think that ways well I don't know, I will be trapped on this side and I will not be able to get back too you, well right focus what you are doing and I will try to killed a few zombies, and Kelly said they are more powerful and then they are much faster, and faster and more gruesome and like to eat kidney and heart and especially brains, oh, yes but don't stay too close to them they were venous you, don't worry about me just worry about yourself, do understand that we are in a city with zombies and they wants us and then Kelly said don't you wants the antidote? Will it work on the zombies? but about you, I am fine and I don't have the infection so I will be okay so will you but don't you hears the sirens are going off and I think that they will blow this town and we will end up being dead. No ways we are going to leave before the blast, but first you need to find a vehicle that works.

I am searching and but I am being follows and I don't like it and I think that you should go inside the candy shop, no ways that I will be stuck in this place do you understand we are both going and we will kick the ass out of the zombies and then we will leave but you, I barely can hears you but what are you saying,? What? Looked out they are coming toward you and run, Kelly I am but they are inches away from you, don't let them bite you don't worry I will not and I will be safe and I did find the key to the car and then we can ride way, and then counted down could be anytime and I don't like this place and situation that the government put in and Kelly started up the engine and then Jeff, came to the car and Jeff wrestle with the zombies about five of them on top of Jeff and Kelly came and pull them off and then Kelly just and then she was trapped and help me and I am coming and I cannot get apart, and I am trying to break away, and then something happened that some soldiers came and shot them with the machine gun and the zombies were dead and now they got into the car and speed away and the soldiers nodded his head and what a mistake they will not make end of town., and they are not thinking and they are going the wrong and bomb are blasting and we cannot get out they have a road block and then Kelly said we need to turned around and then we will be fine, so okay! I agree and then they drove back the soldiers said you need to comes with us right now.

Then the soldiers said well you came back and didn't know that we have an epidemic and I know but I do work for the lab that makes the antidote.

The soldiers smiled and said you both are under quarantine and we are taking you too base, and Kelly said I am not sick or infection and just leave me alone, and were corporation with me, miss, fine, I will.

Later that day, Kelly and Jeff were walking into the base where they test human if they were infection with the virus, and first Jeff went inside and gave his blood and then Kelly, and then she saw her Uncle Fred, and said uncle don't you remember me? Yes you're my niece and what are you doing here, well we were in the streets and they thought were sick, and they bought us here, well release my niece and her friend they were trying to help us and now they are here, and they will not be quarantine. Kelly said thanks Uncle and we need to go into the field and find more zombies and the one that need help, well I cannot release you, for your own protection, so you need to stay here, and then Kelly looked around and said you have a zombies in a fence and the uncle said they will not escape, they will not ,this fence is electric, so it will be safe, yes nothing is safe, don't you know, by now, Uncle if somehow they escape we will get slaughter, you don't want to gets killed, and then do have a plan, about what? In case the zombies break loose? No I don't wants to have this discuss, well fine, Kelly got up and then Jeff said I don't like being here, I don't neither but we have no choice right now.

We will sit and wait for the right moment, and I will tells you and just tonight and then we will walks out, and my uncle will not say a word and he know that I am know how to help to find the virus, and help the sick.

Yes and fight and win the battle and I told you started in 2006 and still fighting and the population is growing and ours population is deceasing, that true, but how do stop them being there meal, well we have killed them off and get ours world back, and what have they done to us, they were once among the living and now we live among the dead. That is true, but what do I do meanwhile, wait for them to eat us up and don't do anything I don't think so, it not going to work.

We will wait until midnight and then we can sneak out about your uncle he can stay here, he should have let us go but he is old man and still fighting and he should just go retired but he refuse because the zombies killed my aunt and he wants to be there! To get even with them because they took her away from him., I will listen to you're going to make it and then I don't know what really going on and then I have a bad feeling and I believe that the zombies are going to break out and then it will be danger and you better to warns them but they don't listen to us, and so they will be sorry if they stay, I saw a few weak about the fence and I think it going to happened tonight, so how do you know?

Out Of Control

The alarms when off and Jeff said how did you know? Did you wreck the fence, now you are accusing me? Solider running and shooting and bomb blowing up and Jeff said it is not good. They are getting closer and they are attacking the soldiers and where is my uncle, well he left this morning and you don't says and he left us to died here, I don't think so, I think that my uncle is infect and you put him into quarantine and then somehow he turned and he just open the fence and they came out and now we are in big battle. Yes, your uncle is a zombie and we had destroy him immediately and I so now your telling me that truth and you need to let us go now, we cannot and then Kelly pointed out the gun and took the jeep and Jeff jump inside and they drove away and soldiers shooting at us and lay low and I am but they kept going and didn't stop even though there is no escape but it will be better than here, that is true, I agree!

They are on the lose and they are very, very hungry and I don't want them to have has a meal, don't worry they will catch you, how you know, you know how they act and do know how this virus started no, they could have eat and drink, and then says if we ate something and we would gets sick and then I don't like that just keeps running but why can we just smash there head and then they were be dead, but looked how many do have to killed? But there are too many for us and I think that we should go to the subway and do think it safe there? I don't know but I think we can find out and hide out and wait until the smoke clear.

"So how many days and how will be survive the underneath it can be dangerous and dark, that true but we have to try to find a way and then we can go to the dock and sail on the yacht and then go to Hawaii and then I think that Maui would be the best place to be right now.

Silent, do you see that they are watching us and they also smell us and I don't like this and I think that they will aim toward us and eat us up.

So are worry to go into the sewer, and walks in underground and then that smell and then what? We get stuck and then we can be in danger and then what it we are not able to go back to the top and running into zombies and in that dim place., I don't think so, I am not going with you but you cannot stay on top you will gets caught, no I will not I will get into the car and drive away and you will leave me in the sewer,, you wanted to go there, and my answer is yes, well I am not going alone and I will go with you, if you don't mind and I don't, and then we will drive out of Los Angeles and go to Michigan, yes and I believe that it cold there and the virus didn't go there, how do you know, I don't , but I am willing to runs down alls the zombies and gets to Michigan and not to deal with zombies, so who told you that location is safe. Well it cold and infection don't spread that quick, well you are, I am a scientist and I do have answer and I need to find a lab and test some items, like what? The water and some organic vegetables, your saying the virus is in the food? Yes I am saying that's! By eating and water it spread like so quickly and they couldn't catch it on time that is your conclusion, yes it is and then Jeff was firing the gun at the zombies, and Kelly said you are a good shot.

I am trying to tell you that the further that we go the better chances, that we will survive this, I know that why we are going to a colder climate,, good, I like it, yes can we go a little faster, so why are we going to Michigan it cold, and that prevent, the spread virus, it does well I am a scientist and I know what goes on and I just think the good idea and it will be right, so I will not fight with you especially when zombies are around and we can end up being zombies, that true, well I think that it will be okay and I trust you, and so we are on our ways.

Silent, but why I think I heard something and I think that we are not alone and so we better keeps driving and no pit shop, I agree, yes, I do. Do you sees the snow falling and snow drift on the street, yes I do and I don't like it very much and we are in a blizzard and we could when to a warm climate and we ended up here and but it freezing cold, and no one around I guess there no zombies, that is a good sign. Yes it you don't think that there not so far no, stop asking me that question about the virus spreading, well I will keep driving and stop but I don't stop the car. No we need to looked around, that is a bad idea, no it not but don't

Jeff, and Kelly said I told you go there because it would be safe, but the weather, Kelly said comes on don't be slow, the street are stranded and they walking, away from the car, and walking and walking and then Jeff said where is the lakes, but Kelly I think that we can stay here for awhile and okay and move on too where? Right now we staying put, do you understanding me, I am and then we need to stay in the hotel tonight, fine and good let looks and then they walks and walks and I don't like it not at all, but you are nagging and you are making me sick, stop it. I will I don't know why I went along with you, I survive without you and I can do it again. What you wants to leave, but I am not going but I am warning you, don't threaten me, I am not, what wrong? I don't like how you're acting; we think that helped each others, is that bad. But it fine you know but we don't have hurried yes we the snow is drifting and it freezing out here, well I see the hotel, about time. About ten minutes and we will steps inside and warm up but the car is too far, it will not be problem.

It won't be no, so times do have to tell you so many, I am annoy with me yes and I am stuck with you, right now but I don't know how long I can take it, stops, stop, I will! They open the door and it abandon and no one around, that is a bad sign, once again your predict that something will happen, like what? About 100 zombies storming in and attack us, I said don't says that's, I won't be negative again, I will try not to talks, silent shut up, and Kelly said I try to be on guard from whom!

Jeff walks out and wanders off and meanwhile Kelly looked and took the key and took the elevator, and went up to the upper floor.

THIN ICE ZOMBIES

Suddenly Kelly looked from the suite and somehow banged the window and Jeff didn't hear the sound and the noise just kept walking and at that time, then they would coming, those zombies would like ice but they wouldn't crack, but more vicious species and more hungry for brains and body parts. Then Jeff saw them, and couldn't believe is eyes that he might not get away but somehow he ran into the ladder, and jump on top and started to climb from building to building and try to reach the hotel and few times Jeff almost fell to the ground, but then got him self up.

Kept on going and didn't stop, about a ten minutes Jeff was inside the hotel found the note and went elevator up, at that moment.

Jeff went to the room, do you sees what you got us in? I didn't know the epidemic, were spread here but you said it would affect in cold air.

But I was wrong, well I didn't this be here but we will be okay, if you says so. But we need too figure out how to get away from ice zombies and they are viscous and starving and they wants our brain and I am not going to give up and I am going to beat them do you understand and I do and we will get out of here but don't you sees a blizzard out there, yes but we still going to take a chance and then we will get back to LA, but LA is no different than here, but we don't have to deal with Ice Zombies the worst source of means kind and dangerous species, and I just don't wants to find out, do you understand? Yes I do and I just want to leave now, fine, I think it not the right time to go looks at so many of them.

Yes I know but if we stay it will be more dangerous and it time to go into the storm and heading west. but why not east.

Later that day, Jeff looked around on the streets and called out and said they move on the other side of town, are you sure and then they went to the car and it didn't wanted to start and said we better start moving, don't why, don't you sees them, yes,, they are headed our ways.

All right! But once again the car wouldn't start and then it did and then they drove away and then they just kept going and they down town a dozen of zombies and but there will be more ahead and it was more than a thousand, and then the other side would more zombies and I notice that they were not the same species and then mean and more aggressive and wants brains non stops.

Then they took the right turn and then they headed on the highway and they were relief about getting out of dodge, so we are and now we might be safe not at this time and I think when we are complete out of this highway and this city, that is what I wants but it is taking too long.

About two hours they were in the clear and but the snow was falling and it was windy and drifting and I couldn't believe what was going on!!!

In the midnight we stop for a rest and sat there for a while and seems calm but it was a totally mistake, and we just took off and drove away and didn't looked back. But are you contagion, no I am not and I just want to get away from here now and I tired of being in this nightmare and I just wants to go, I am going and I sorry to told you too comes here and I just want to go to a warm climate and I just don't want to run into the ice zombies and they are ugly and vicious looking creature, that is true, zombies kept following us that day and I couldn't believe that the zombies were much faster and not slow type and they wanted to catch us and then I told Jeff and Kelly said, how long before we are out of Michigan and then we started to head to Chicago, and it also cold there and I just don't wants to stop there neither and I just don't want to get infection and contagion of the virus and think we will make it through the epidemic and but don't nagged about the situation and remember what they said don't too touch anyone and don't eat the foods that was open, okay! Then they pass by Chicago headed to the Maine and Vermont and New Hampshire, and Kelly still complain about the cold, and we will deal with the ice zombies, how do you know I don't but I just don't like it and there are alls type of zombies and I believe the worst one are the ice ones, and I never knew that they were around but now I know and the other zombies, are less effective and but these are more advance, and about the one that are mix with the vampire/ zombies, they are also very dangerous and I don't want to run into those neither, well the whole population is danger and I think that we need to be caution and then be on your guard, yes I am and we are in the car and we are going fast enough and then but are we going to fill up it there is power at the pump and I hope it does and I don't wants be stranded with these zombies and me and I but we have no choice and I know that it is not airborne and but they said it was in the foods and water, so we cannot eat or drink that food might be containment and so we need to find some kind of source of food supply that we need to live and then they kept on going and going and then Kelly said, and then Jeff said I am really hungry and we need to stop at the restaurant and but they are not open and so we just had to keeps on going and not giving up that somewhere out there was more the living and not the living dead and then Jeff just stop the car and when out and start to walks and I came out and said what are you doing? You want to get killed? No I just wants to eat, and you are risking our life, yes I am but I am not going to starve to death and I just want to you too stops, why they are coming and you will be bitten by them, I cannot take this anymore, said Jeff, now you are sounding like a coward, but I know that your not,, I am glad that you said that, but don't denied it, you are taking chances and I don't like to be in the middle and so come back to the car and then just keeps going. I cannot I just wants to eat and eat a cook meal and not fighting with zombies.

Well we can just walking and nowhere and now Kelly said well

NOWHERE TO RUNS OR HIDE!
BATTLE

CONTAGION DAY 1

Do you know what we are walking through? Yes we are in the middle of the epidemic, and the contagion was worst walking over the dead bodies that were venous by the zombies and Jeff you bought me here and I cannot believe that you did and we were safe and Jeff said not exactly,, what do you means that every location has zombies, and there is no help to comes and save us,. How do you know that's! Looked there was a tank in the middle of street and zombies approaching us and we didn't have no place to hide but I pull Jeff and told him to hide under the tank and Jeff and I. this time it was a close called and then they were trying to grab us and then somehow we got up and ran fast and went toward the car but they were standing and now we need to knock them down and then the siren went off, and meant that military were heading this ways and they are going to shoot us, they will think that we are zombies, yes I know. But they stood for awhile and then we got into the car and drove away. later that day and then they ran out gas, and started walks and walks and saw a abandon building and they went inside and they shut the door and then lights came on and the tank and military vehicle were on that street and you heard shooting and then splatter bodies alls over and then Kelly said I don't like this place but we have too be silent and don't let them hears us, because we probably were gets shot, no kidding and now we are stuck inside some building that we might be alone and hope there are no zombies inside. But they started to walks up to the top of the roof and they saw helicopter flying over the head and then suddenly they were shooting at us and then we bend down, hide and looking around and hiding out.

Now we will stay put, and not to go outside but, we cannot go run outside, because we will gets shot in the head and I think that should just

58

go hide for now and wait until they leaves, but we don't know when that going to be, sure I know but we need to be patience and then we will sneak out and run and run for your life, yes and then we can be safe in some sense and then we can just get out of this place and then we can just go, silent I hears someone, I hears voices, sound like they are going to close this place and how the hell we will gets out by the basement and that might be with a bunch of zombies and then what? Now you are making me sick., and then we need to continue and going out of here immediately, good I don't want to be here in the first place but you started to wander off and then they are stuck here and I don't like it and I think that now it is the time to move., your right!

Later that night, Jeff and Kelly snuck out and they when outside and it was clear and then we just looked around and then we were safe that what I thought, but it they came and then zombies came toward us and bomb blowing up and then we just ran and ran away and didn't looked back, that days. But the contagion got worst and there was roadblocks and seem like we had to jump in the cold river.

DONT THINK THAT THEY ARE IN THE RIVER? No I don't think so I think that we are safe right now, but for how long, I don't have answers but I think the river is a good idea, but why because it cold and wet, we will FREEZ, STOP SAYING THAT, RIGHT NOW! Fine but it is true and I don't want to go to that chilly water I refuse, well you have two choice jumps into the water or the zombies will get you, well I chose to jump into the water. Fine, just don't stand there I won't! about a minute later they were in the water and it was really cold and they swam to the shore and got out and Kelly said now I need a blanket and then I am really cold and I don't like it and I don't neither, thanks but I did save ours lives today, sure you did but still I am cold. STOP THIS NON SENSE, AND LISTEN TO WHAT I AM SAYING! I am trying but it is really difficult to do so when you are soak wet, I am too and don't complain, I am trying to be patience but I am cold and then Jeff came up to her and hold her tight and now are you warm? Yes I am thanks this body temperature, sure it is, I know.

Jeff and Kelly walks and then they saw the house and said let go there now, okay I agree, and they both when inside, and resting a bit before the zombies came around, and then they heard banged and the noise outside, I thought we got away but once again we are surrounded by them, that what happened when a epidemic hit and everyone is effective, that is true I work in the lab and I know that some just didn't get sick but they got bitten and then they became ZOMBIES. even though in the lab it happened, that true, but this is not really the one day of contagion since 2006 in a small lab in New Mexico and it spread to LA and alls over and that why we cannot control it but it is getting out hands and so I don't understand when it going to stop.

But they do not know exactly how this all started and I think that we should gets back to civilization and then we can cope with the problem much better and then we can survive this situation, yes I agree and I think that we should not be traps and then we can just keeping going and have the battle of the lifetime., yes. This been going on for a long time and it is not going to stops and there will be no end of this virus and I think that we are the only one left and then but we need to beat them and they cannot win, do you understand what I am saying I when through this before and I think I will do it again, but looks how many there are, I don't care I am going not giving up and I don't want you neither, do you understand? Yes I do but Jeff, we cannot lose this battle and this were be end of human being to be alive., and the only were walks this earth were be zombies and I am going to prevent this epidemic to win and I am going to the lab and working on a antidote and then we might have a chance of survive, that is true. But meanwhile we need to go and find a lab. But where do we go? I don't know but we need to find it now.

Searching for a lab for the cure to save the population and if there are anyone alive of course but if not we are on own ways and so I don't like this scenario and it looked bleak and I think that so far we are lucky and luck can run out and I know that I don't want that's I know but we have no choice but keeps moving and finding a safe place with a lab and I can work on XZ 12 and that was the last antidote that I work on but it can save some of the symptoms and then I can work on a stronger dose and do think it will work I need to go back to LA and back to my lab and looked up the notes, but we are still fighting with the zombies but we need to by pass and then find a lab and that is very important and I know. Meanwhile Jeff started to looked around and Kelly thought he was not that education like she was but, Kelly needed him has much has he needed her and so it was a good relationship to a point but there days that they argument with the vital about living and not dying at this time, and trying to beat the zombies and getting the formula from the lab but that will be a long journey and then it will difficult of working on the antidote and then, Kelly just wander at this time if it was worth it.

But Kelly kept a lot to herself and Jeff knew that Kelly was up too something and then, stop in the middle of road and said "comes and get me" are you crazy and they do smell you, I know but I just want to get some fiber and then some blood from that one lady zombie and seem like she not going to bite me but, well I will have the gun pointed toward you and then if she tried to bite you don't worry and then Jeff pull out the gun and Kelly and said well now I will approach her and then I will gets the blood and then the fiber and test on the kit that I have but watch your step and I am and don't let me get caught and eaten up by them meanwhile that you are just putting us in dangerous and then you says it might work and then you said could works, so what is it? wait, let me prick her finger, well it really stupid., no it is scientist and you just want the blood, yes and I do want reserve the process, well it just work this way go up to the subject and reject and then get the blood and then you test and some of the kit might be positive but I will work on many subject.

So how many subject and many blood sample to need test and then run it and then I will have the conclusion, well is that good and then we will be able to get rid of them, and then we will have ours home back, that is true, yes and I were not lies, so that why that what I am kind of risking so to save our lives, and then they came too close that Jeff pull out the knife and stab the zombie and then a whole bunch were there once again, and Jeff and Kelly was in back of him and then Kelly got into the car and Jeff pass it and then turned around and then ran for to the car and when inside and said we are getting the hell out of this place and said yes we are so they sped out and then they drove over the high bridge and then got close to LA but Jeff said I am not going into the city, I am not going alone, so we are sticking together, do you understand? Yes, I do.

Well, I sees a town near this city and we should crash there for awhile and then we can just rest and take a shower, but you don't know we cannot rest we need to be on guard, do you understand, I been through a lot and I do realized what you are saying and then we can just fight, and later that night thought they were alone in that hotel, suddenly Kelly was seeing different faces and then I woke up and said where is Jeff, well he is around, I wants to sees him, no you cannot sees him, what did you do to him, nothing and at that moment I was scare to death what they might do to me, so about a minute later, one of the stranger was on top of me and then I just wanted to push him off, but then Kelly decided not too! About a minute later I saw Jeff was tight up and I couldn't get to him but I thought to myself if I am able to escape then I were sneak out and not too be seen, I thought it was a good plan but I notice that I was naked needed to find clothes and steal a weapon and then run, and I had no clue where I was at this point and I didn't know where Jeff when?

But I lay still and looking and I saw mores than one faces and I didn't know them, and I now I would somehow get some clothes and then get the gun and run out in the cold, so I did but I really didn't wanted to leave Jeff behind, but at this time I had no choice I needed to get help and escape Jeff, now I got dressed and snuck out, and then walks out and then I walks near the edge near the water and into the alley and I kept going and I didn't stop but I knew that I was not alone. But they were following at first I thought I were fall into the water and at that point I was terrify and I didn't stop but kept going, and but they were getting near but they had ugly faces and I thought at first they were zombies but they were not, but I think they were Jeff friend that just when wild and they just didn't like that he bought me here, and he was like a reject, by them now.

Now they wants me to be there baby machine but I just ran and I kept running and I didn't know what town I was now I knew that I would run into zombies, in case I believe that I were be more safer inside and probably they were not come into that location but they still were in back of me but I couldn't lose them, and I just felt trapped and I just kept going and I don't know how this going end up but I am not going to gets caught that is my safe bet at this point and I just was scare and also brave, and then I saw a store and I snuck inside and I hide in the corner in the dark spot and no lights shining, so now I try not to make a sound.

I was very quiet and not being seen and then I saw stairs and I went toward them and I try not to being seen and then I when upstairs and then I when into one of the room and I looked out of the window and I just peek out and then I looked but they still looking for me, and then I saw Jeff walking with them, and I wanted to scream out but Jeff was one of them and he just wanted me to believe that he was the victim.

CONTAGION DAY 3

Jeff called out his friends and said I know how she think and she could be hiding in one of these houses and we need to find her and then we can fertile and she can have our children, that why I hook up with that person, Kelly, oh I though you had a thing for her, well she is very smart and she is a scientist and well she know how do make the antidote and then she can make us well, I think that I do have the virus and she is very important and we need to find her immediately, I hear you, loud and clear but why did you jump into her face and attacking, and you have scare her, well we make a mistake, yes we did. But we will fix it when we locate her and then we can help her find a lab and then she make the antidote, and then we will have sex with her and take turns, I don't think so, but why you are her protection? No but she save me a lot of times from the zombies and she is very vital to our mission, I think that you are right! Meanwhile Kelly kept low and make sure not one would sees her and she stay in that apartment above the store, and was quiet like a mouse. Later that day Kelly looked around and it was safe., put the water on took off her clothes and step into the shower and washed her up and then got dressed up with blue jean and sweatshirt and put boots and had the pistol and put into her pocket and looked around for bullets and now she was ready to beat ass with the boys and she knew, what to do and how get rid of the gang of Jeff and then gets even with Jeff and then would leave him to the zombies, to defend without a weapon to even the score.

Now I need to helped Jeff even though he left me with those goon and now they left him without a weapon to fight the zombies and I need him and save him and even he is not the bests friend right now but I can help me to get the lab and also I saw those three women staring at me and

I don't want to be caught this could be plan to trap me so I need to be very careful to approach Jeff, and they might just wanted to get me back but I also don't understand why those women are helping those men. So how I do get to him and then save him, I don't have a clue, right now but I think that I should just go and not think and it might not be traps, then it could be. Now it was getting darker and darker and I didn't like where I was standing so I got into the light and they saw me and they started to chase me and I didn't know which ways to go. But then I ran up to Jeff and I untied him and he said, why did you save me just run for your life, and I don't wants you here and I am sorry what I have done, Kelly just kept running and the zombies started to roam near her and she was close to be bitten and then Jeff shot the zombie and Kelly got inside the car and drove away and then Kelly decided to turn around and pick up Jeff and then she stop the car and he said why? Did you stay, you are in danger, I don't care, and I wanted to help you even though you betray, me I do understand why? But I don't want to be alone. Fine, let go now, okay!

Two days later the contagion was near gone and they were near LA and Jeff was relief that the enemies that he knew didn't catch up and then Kelly when to the end of town to the lab, and when inside the building, and when on her floor and then Jeff said what should I do? Well you found me the paperwork and then I will get the test tube, then I will mix the formula, then I will heat up to the right temperature, and then I will need a subject and then maybe you can be one, well I don't wants to get infection, well this could be the answer for the epidemic, and then we will go town and to town to cure the sick. I am not going close to the zombies, that are totally sick, no it is not, that the only that we will survive this battle are you should? Yes I am right about this, well you are assurance about it very much, yes I am in my environment, but you feel out of place how do you know that because how you reaction to this whole situation, fine leave me alone, okay don't touch anything, I won't!

Suddenly it got dark and Jeff said what going on and I don't know, and it is pitch blackout and because the moon got cover because it really dark out of there, and I need a flashlight I don't know if I cannot find it but hurried and I will drop it and I don't wants to spill it and I just wants us to be okay and so far I don't know what I am doing and I don't wants to mix the wrong formula, otherwise might be wrong and backfire, I totally understand, and but I missing the item that is not here and we need to leave this lab and go into grocery store and pick up spinach, are you kidding? Nope, serious, well I don't like taking risk but you must go now and get the fresh spinach and the whole and I need to cook it and then put into the tube and then mix in the machine and then I will give too you, thanks, I am the guinea pig, yep I have no other subject here.

Later that night Jeff snuck out and looking around and it was clear and then Jeff find the store and then when inside it was wide open and didn't realizes that zombies might be inside but just walk in and looked around and find the spinach and walks out and then was being follow by the zombies, and now Jeff was getting worry but I ran for my life and then I got to the building where Kelly was locate and then I when inside and then I when up and carry the bag of spinach and I hope it was enough to make the antidote and I walk in and Kelly was like fast asleep.

About a minute, I woke up and then Kelly said did you gets it and I said yes I did and I hope I bought enough, and I looked and then Kelly that fine for now, and then Jeff sat down and Kelly said well now I need to focus, just sit back and then Jeff just fell asleep and then Kelly said I am ready to test you, now, let me sleep. And you won't get infection but you will be immune, yes I do understand. Then Jeff sat down and Kelly gave too him and he just had a bad reaction and she had to calm him down and said don't worry, I will make you feel better, just relax.

About one hour later., Jeff was up and feeling fine and Kelly was testing his blood and it was getting normal and just rest., okay!

EPIDEMIC END

Jeff was refreshing and feeling fine and not weak now we need to go out to the field, okay. Yes but we need to go underground and through the tunnels and reach the end of town, and find out the one are a bit sick, and give them a shot, then we will survivors need to help them immediately and I do know that is very vital circumstance and they will try to prevent us to do that's ! I do understand! But we need to keeps going and then the earth shook and Kelly said did we have a earthquake I think that we did and I don't like this because the zombies are going to grow and then there will be no stopping them, I do hears what you are saying but I just don't know if we are going to beat them. But you saying we that still there is an epidemic going on? Yes and they might be saying it is over but it is not seems like there is no end to this but I am immune from the virus, yes you are and now we need to find more persons and help them, sure and one more time it shook and then Jeff fell and then Kelly pick him up and said are you okay? Yes about you? I am also okay.

Now they walks and walks and until end of the line and then they got outside and Kelly said now I am going to save more peoples and then it will be back to normal and then we can beat the zombies, do think that going go help them, yes, yes, and then I will feel that I did my job and those peoples were sick and now they will be well, but Kelly don't know if it working, well I gave you and it showing that you are immune and you will not become the " night of the living dead" and so it working and I am glad and so now we are in the street and looked for the one that foam at the mouth and then catch them,, do think that I am crazy and catch a zombie, and probably get bitten, lady you are totally crazy and I don't like your method but it sure help me but I am not going to be a target.

Well fine, I will catch the ZOMBIES, and you just can looks and what I am doing and you have no reason that you will dies, well you might wants too get revenge at me, because I betray you too my friends, well I am not the low life likes you, Jeff, well I try to tells that we should have gone someplace different but you still force my hand and so I bought you to my friends and they wanted to have sex with you and they also have betray me and that why you save me., yes that is true otherwise you were been dead meat about five hours ago but you are alive and kicking, yes , because of you, yes, yes, yes, don't says it and rub in and I won't be I do need your help for get the sick to me and I won't let them bite you, I will keeps my word. I am trying to trust you but it is really hard too, because in the past my friends did double cross me and so I don't trust anyone., so you have caught me a lesson of trust and now I do not trust you what you says or do, thanks a lot, I will not let you down, okay!

Meanwhile Kelly walks in front of him and Kelly said watch your steps and they might just jump out and gets you and I will be ready with the syringe and then I decided to spray the whole territory and we need to hide inside and then I will put it on full power, so that mean that you need to go back to the lab, yes and you watched the door and I will sneak in and then you hide in the corner, and I will and make sure that you lock the door shut and then it will not affect you, then she said here is a mask and it will protection and make sure it does not have a hole that air were get inside you, yes I do and I do, then Kelly reach the floor of the lab and check it out and put on the machine and make sure that the windows were shut tight and then she called Jeff on the speaker and Kelly now had warns him now go inside that room and Kelly said now, and he nodded his head and said to Kelly, I am fine do it and they are trying to gets inside, hurried before it is too late, I am but the switch were not turn on and now Kelly was in a panicked and but didn't make sound that she was not then Jeff said what wrong? Nothing and then the outdoor were being spray and Jeff got out of the room and came upstairs to Kelly and she said why did comes, I didn't tell you it was okay. Well I didn't wants to be alone, well you took a big risk on both of us, thanks again but it seems like it is working and they are falling to the ground and I don't what going to happen again but we are secure, do hears what I am saying, yes.

I think that we are out danger but it will take about 24 hours to know and then they we will process more of the spray into the air and sees what will go on with the epidemic, well it is not foolproof but still it some kind of cure for not the totally contagion person but some percentage will be cure, I am glad to hears about my friends that are out here, I don't know but if they were sick, they will be better, depend how long that they had the illness, thanks! Are watching them,, yes and I think something happening and I think that they we will not become zombies, at this point we need to watch and stay back and not be sees or heard, fine I will just wait for what you says and I will not step out and make us notice., that is no, no, and no, and okay! I need to do some blood works on you and make sure that there is no error,, fine take my blood and then Kelly did and test it on the test tube and then the reading looks good and that good said Jeff and now Jeff was relief and sat down and Kelly was mix stuff and then Kelly took a sip and drank it and then Jeff said what did you take? Well I had to test myself and I think it will not harm me, well don't care that you are the only that will save the world, well in my job you need to take risk so I have and now we wait and sees what happen and then I will write you instructions in case that you have to give me a shot, no why did you do this, well I am trying to help so I need to find out the red cell and white cell and then the killer cells, well so it were take about ten minute, if my mood change or I just fall down and or my eyes rolls.,, you take the blue needle and put into my arm in five minute, and then ten minute later if it does not work you give me the red shot of the needle and then wait for one hour and then take some blood and test it under the test tube, well if nothing happened then you have nothing to worry about , thanks!

Experiment Procedure

One hour later, Jeff was watching Kelly and seems all right! At that moment Jeff was relief, and then he notice that she was acting not like herself, and now Jeff was wandering what to do next. Do I follow the procedure by step by steps and or I just jump into the red needle shot, and then he read the instruction and saw underline over one hour might save the subject and were not turn but first follow the procedure from step one and then wait and sees and then reject the second shot, and now Jeff was wandering what next and he just did what Kelly told him to do and then two hours Kelly woke up from a deep sleep and sounded like herself but one thing that she wanted to eat him, and he push her away. Then he looks into her eyes and then they were not looking strangely and then she was complete herself and now Kelly asked how I was? Very close to being a zombie, well did you take blood work; I am doing the test now. Later that night, they went out to the field and they search for survivor and it was difficult that point. I believe it is not foolproof and I think the syrupy will still not work totally but I think there is a chance, nothing is a sure thing so, maybe some will make it and some won't that is the scenario, okay and when they were walking in the tunnel, Kelly knew that they were not alone and then Kelly said they are in back of us and I think that we will be okay and they are not fast but they will move a bit faster, and then Jeff said are we going to get caught? I don't know but I do have cure and if I am able to give the shot before they died, then they will not become zombies, but if they died, then they will become zombie.

Later that day, somehow they reach end of the tunnel and it looks like a cell and they are unable to open, and then what are we going to do? Right now to break through and not get caught, well it is a jail cell and we don't have the key and we do have a problem and don't panic, Jeff we will be fine, how do you know well, I still have syringe, and one shot for one zombie, and then we would leave, but that we would not help us and I don't know understand what your saying., well I think it will works out and it will be okay, trust me., well I hope that it will be fine.

About ten minute they were coming toward and now what gets your gun out and shoot them now and I am but the gun is jammed, then try again and then shot more zombies. then Kelly stood still and was like in a trance and panic looks and what wrong with you, well I don't know but the pressure and I cannot take it, what then she was froze and then Jeff said don't do this to me, I need you help me, okay, I am trying and I think this battle is getting me and I cannot handle it, then the first shot and then two zombies fell and then Jeff said more are coming and then Kelly took out the spray and started to spray the air and then zombies were falling to the ground and about ten minute we will sees, if it is working, got it, but. Jeff you need to feel there hands. I am not going to do, myself. Okay I will be on your side. Promise that you will not run, fine I won't trust me, I am. Jeff walks up to one of the zombie and pull him to the left and then Kelly then him the shot and then we will wait and sees what happening and then we will do more of them if it is too late, and then we will leaves the tunnel and go on top and do the same has we are doing here, and that is such idiot idea and but I am willing to save the population and what the government destroy, yes I do understand what you are saying, but don't argue with me, I am not but I believe that I am doing the right job to save and not be killed by zombies, but you are trying to beat the system too, someway yes and I don't understand your knowledge but I think that we will make it, at last your taking what I am saying serious, and it is working and the epidemic, it will take about one hour to two day that show the symptom are gone, then my job will be over and everything will be normal, that sound good, and I agree with you, and then more zombies are coming and then it is too late for these guys so we have to shoot them in the head, that sound awful and I don't like it.

About five day later, Kelly said I will runs out and I will need to get back to the lab and make much more, and you will watched the doors and windows that they don't break inside, yes, Kelly I will do it and you have promise me,, that you will not doze off and sleep this is very vital, do understand, but the crisis are not over,, when will it be? I don't know it the spray in the outside working or not, but the conclusion is that we are kind of winning the battle, that is a relief and I will be able to go home to my family, that is a slim chance, at this moment but I don't doubt it at alls.

Jeff sat and it was time to return to the lab but they had to watch there steps and then make sure not get capture by the zombies, and most of alls not to gets bitten, but Kelly said one more time to visit the lab and then we will go outside and fight the battle and use the antidote and then survive this zombies epidemic, and I don't like being in the middle of it, I don't neither, they got inside and then Jeff kind was falling asleep and then Kelly shook him and said stay wake and watch the doors, I am no you are not! About two minute later the zombies were trying to break in and so where is the rifle, on the side of the door, well okay! Jeff was not really happy about what was going on and then Kelly said well I think it will hold with the steel wall door and they will not be able to get inside and then we will have to fight with when we need to get back to the basement and then into the tunnel and get the hell out of here.

I know, I know but I we will, but follow me to the basement and then to the outside, great and leave this awful and not going back that was a bad idea I agree. Then the formula was done and they left the lab.

They walk out and killed and getting to the basement then the generator.

Generator stop and the lights started to flicker off and on then it got pitch black, and then they use the flashlight and glow and shadow on the walls.

Then the zombies would come toward us, and now Jeff said we will die.

ZOMBIES IN DARK TUNNEL

We will died in this tunnel we could have out of here but now we are surrounded, by zombies and bitten by them and I don't want to be on floor, you won't be dead you won't be, take my word, I am but quiet I hears something, I hears peoples talking, you must be kidding.

About five minutes, the door open I saw a blond man and a dark lady with black hair, and they were tall but they had a shotgun, and the woman with tattoos, on her arm and near her breast.

One was one skull and one with little red heart with an arrow sticking out near breast, and the man with tattoos had an America flag and a name Lisa on his arm. The man and woman pull his up too the top before the zombies try to attack us, and now I was relief that we would save by strangers, Kelly said to Jeff I am safe, are we not sure but then they thanks them, and then they got into the truck and drove away. wait, wait then they speed off and then the rain came and it was dark and mist and couldn't sees anything in front of you and it was awful and I thought we were doomed but we were lucky one more time, and then we were in a heading out of town and I did wanted to help more the sick but the stranger said we need to keep going and we headed out of LA to Seattle and going over the bridge and then I said what is your name, and then man answer, Mark, and she my friend is called Jessie, and where did you comes from well we are from Minnesota, and Mark is from Texas and we met up when the epidemic started in 2006, and we were searching for peoples and we are glad that we find you. So are we! That is the relief that we are coping right now and we were afraid that we were the only one life, well your not and they are still fighting with the zombies and don't know when it going to end. They spoke about life was and how it is now and then how things are getting better, said Jessie and Mark and they miss there family and how the contagion that so many death and the only ways to get rid of this just burn the zombies, yes and shoot them in the head, yes that is true. But Jessie you don't looks well what wrong, well I think that I am pregnant with Mark child but the child might be infection, why do says that's! I was sick for one day and then I find out that I was going to have a baby, and I am about three month, and you need to take the antidote, and Jessie said I am not going to harm my child with the shot, are crazy, no but I do love my baby and I don't wants it too died. But it will not harm you and not the baby neither, I don't believe you. Then she said to Mark tell her stop nagging me, I will! Mark warns Kelly stop this and don't harass her, fine.

They kept driving and driving and they stop for fuel and got more gas and drove away before they got stamped by Zombies.

About one hour and they stop into the local hotel and then said why this place? Well easy access to leave and the car in front of the hotel in case that we need to leave early, good idea. So they staying, yes but Mark and Jessie, telling Kelly and Jeff not go inside and she said why not?

Later that had a battle with the battle and it was not a losing battle and but don't let them, I won't let them in but they are very hard to stop and they are really vicious and I don't like what I we are in this situation and then what are we going to do? Well shut this place tight, seems like you wanted to us to be here and you must be kidding, but I am not and it will be a difficult task, and but we have enough weapons but we need to get the helicopter pad and take it out of Seattle, well my mission to help the sick but they are unable, to help beyond help, well you saying they are zombies and the cure will not work that is correct. So I just let them become zombies and then we shoot them in the head and, that is the solution, yes that is not the answer to Kelly to Jessie, the population will grows and I don't wants that's! I don't neither but we have no choice, yes we do, I can just give them the remedies and then they will not turned and how do you know? Well, but meanwhile the zombies are outnumber and I don't like it, well we need to get the hell out of here now, said the tattoo girl to Kelly, and you don't realize our lives are in danger, would stay and risk your own life, or fight and get to the helicopter and get the hell out of here? Well, I don't know but we are wasting time and we need to go now,, but there are thousand of zombies out there,, and if we step out we need to maneuver and have a idea to get around them, I put I don't know it will works,, but I am willing to try.

About one hour later, they alls step out and the zombies, the tattoo girl

Jessie walks out and Kelly warns her, don't go now, but she didn't listen to them and make things worst for them but Jessie kept walking and walking and toward the zombies and Jeff ran out and now he was in the middle of the street and Mark when out with his sword and then Kelly with the shotgun and they were blasting the zombies and Kelly said move over and don't let them grab you, I won't but they were like a inch away and it was really scaring and that I were be next to dies, no you won't , I will save you, you will, thanks, said the Jessie to Jeff and then they were all together and then Kelly said well what should I do next? Stay I will comes closer but then a few zombies got into the middle of them and the battle began and Kelly was really furious and I don't like that Jessie got us into this situation and now we need to killed off the zombies, and I was to exhausted about fighting, but we need to get to that helicopter and yes we do but you were so stupid, and then Mark said don't called my girlfriend stupid but she is, well she just didn't wanted to stay and be trapped, now we are trying to stay alive, and I know but I am very worry what going on, me too! But they are near me and I am scare that they will bite me and I don't want to end of dead, you won't don't let them smell you and walks very slowly and calm

NOWHERE TO RUN OR HIDE!
BATTLE

IN THE MIDDLE OF ZOMBIES

Jessie called out and Kelly said don't do this, you are getting yourself notice and they will bite you and eat your brain, no why did I run out here and not protection. But you didn't listen to what I was saying but you still when out and now you are stuck and if you move quick and they will grab you, so move very slowly, I am but they are looking at me, I cannot help at this point of time, but just stand still and move toward me, and walks but not run, and then reach Jeff, hand and then he will pull you out in the middle of the street and then we will go at the end of the street and go into that car and head out of here, but then Jeff said well you the antidote in the hotel, and Kelly said I am not going back inside because if I do, then I will be trapped, any minute that Jessie was going to be fine but now she put the group into a jeopardy and Kelly didn't like what she did and now they had maneuver from there very quickly and they got into the car and headed to the airport,, and get a helicopter and leave Seattle., and then a few minute later, they saw falling stars and then Kelly notice that it was going to be a moon eclipse, and that is not a good sign,, said Kelly to Jeff, but why it bring mores zombies to life, no, yes so we better hurried, and I am so what now,, silent I am thinking what to do next.

So, we got into the car and drove but then Jessie said well I need to get back into the hotel and Jeff and Kelly said well we are not going back do you understand? Well it is very important, but what is it? Well it is maps that tell us where the safe zone is? Well we were not in the safe zone so we were in a danger area and I don't says that we just keeps on going and then Mark pull out the gun and said turn around this instantly or I will blow your head off, Jeff said you will not shoot her, try me but you need her and she knows a lot about the epidemic, well maybe I should shoot you,

78

you need both of us, not really, then Jeff said Mark put the gun down, so Jeff decided and turns the car around and heading back to the hotel. Jeff drove to the hotel, Jessie got out of the car. Ran inside and got the map, the corner of her eyes. Zombies were getting closer and closer, about inches away and open the ran into and heard the zombies, start saying, we will say, "we wants brains" do you hears that's? Yes so turn the car and get the hell out of here, now!

Sped out and now they were following us and at the moment one jump on the back of car and window smash and one of zombie grab Jessie and she hit with the stick but fighting for her life, but then Jeff help Jessie, and pull out the gun and start to shoot, then the zombie fell from the car and saw the blood dripping out the head and the rest of zombies pull out the brain and gut from the zombie, and Jessie said well now we don't have to worry, they are back there and they got closer to the airport.

Suddenly stop and zombies would at the airport, now what?

But we need to continue head to the air strip, and we will get on the small plane, well I thought we would go to take the copter, change of plan.

What I thought we would taking the helicopter, but now the small plane to fly to an island. I thought we would go, to the island like Australia, but that not island, I know but we need to stop at Hawaii, and headed to Australia, I heard that it is not infection with the virus and we will gets help.

So they approach the plane and check out the plane, and Jessie was a bit reckless and careful and letting the zombies seeing her and they would behind the fence and then the chain broke and few zombies were coming toward us and then Jessie jump into the plane, they all got inside, Jeff started up, the engine and the plane was on the runway and in few minutes, they were in the air, now they were happy and relief and then the engine stop, and then it start again, and plane nose went down that moment they thought they would crash. But Jessie was freaking out and saying we are going to dies, no we are not dying today. Then they level down and headed forward and into the cloud, and then the rain and wind and it was thunder lighting, and then it was really severe storm, and some mist came and Jeff didn't sees where they headed, about four hours, they were fast asleep, and Jeff was about to sleep and Kelly came inside and said don't sleep, I am not. Then she pulls his cap off and gave him a kiss and then he put auto pilot and they make love.

About one hour later they would getting closer to Hawaii and then Jeff said get dress and now I need to check the radar and level of the plane, and we can neck later, that great, yes I am in love with you, so do I know.

Then Kelly went to her seat but Jessie got up and went to see Jeff and lock the door and took her tee shirt and then she grab him and touch his penis and rub it and then Jeff said stop touching me, and push her away and ran back to the seat and cried rape, and Kelly said he didn't touch you and now your lying to your teeth all about rape. Then Mark got up and said I will beat is his ass, well now your boyfriend will beat up the pilot and what will be end up in the mountain crash because Jeff didn't wants to get on with you. I will stop you bitch before you killed us alls, do you understand what I am saying,, yes but he did rape, that is a fucking lies, and don't get on my nerve I will beat your ass, you tattoos girl and it was much better without you both, I should open the door and threw you both out of the plane, well Missy don't be such a smart ass, Jessie and Mark we will threw you out first and Jeff would not even know, try me. I will you bitch, stop calling me names, well it is the truth. Five minutes later Jessie and Kelly were about to fight and Jeff said okay time to put on your seat belt and stay put it is time to Land in Hawaii, and Jessie, well aren't you lucky, I thought I was going to threw you in the ocean, but now we will land and then we can fight on the ground. You better believe and I cannot wait to beat your ass, so tough girl shown me what you have, fine, you think I am not tall and I don't have the muscle and not able kick ass watched me tattoo girl, and your threaten don't scare me, well they should, come on show what you got? Fine I will and I will not hesitate.

REVENGE

The plane landed and Kelly got out and so did Jessie and they started with the fist and Kelly got a black eyes and then Kelly knock her down on the ground and then once again Kelly punch her into her stomach, but she kept fighting and at that moment, the guys called out and said stop fighting, and they nodded the head and said no, and then Jeff said looks the zombies are headed this ways hurried come in and then, Kelly pick up Jessie and they when inside the plane and then Jeff started the engine and they were headed up to the sky, and they were relief, and that was really close but we don't have too much fuel to fly, well that not great! No it is not. Now where are we going to go here but different side oh I sees, once again your boyfriend is be bossing again, be quiet so argument, let her stop nagging me, okay I will. Girl, girl stop argue with each others and we have other this to deal with and not accusing each others we have zombies out there and the plane, and flew over the water and then it started to have engine trouble and then once again, seem like the plane was going down and Jeff, was saying stay in your seat, and we are, but where are we headed, away from the north shore, and heading to Maui.

"Do you think it will be safe, and at that moment the plane when down to the water and somehow they were able to escape and now they swam to the shore but they were still in Oahu, and I don't like this and I don't know where the airport is located and I think we better find a plane and get the hell out of here and I am soak and so are we.

We need to find a hotel and find dry clothes and then we can go and find a helicopter to fly to Maui, don't you sees they are in the water too, I cannot believe my eyes, they are so what are we going to do, just keeps walking and find a path to the hotel and hide out there for awhile, well that is a good idea, for now but how do we distract them for the escape, well I have some fireworks and some grenade and it might work, but do think that Australia will be safe place? I don't know how to answer that's. But I think so, well you are taking chances with ours lives, I know with mine too, so we need to get into the outrigger hotel now, fine we will.

They walks for about five miles and Jessie decided to looked around and they didn't sees if she was along but then she when straight to the beach and found a blanket and lay it down and took off her blouse and underneath Jessie had her bath suit and lay down on the blanket and meanwhile, Kelly and Jeff and Mark when inside the lobby to the desk and took a key and when to the penthouse but then Kelly said to Mark, and said where is Jessie, I thought she was with us and I didn't notice that she was missing, Jessie like to lay on the beach, and Kelly said well she does not understand that there are ZOMBIES out there, well she just absent minded, well I were called her stupid and crazy, that she is too.

But I need to find her and I think that I know where she went so I will go and find her, fine. Then you can yell at her and tell her that we need to stick together, do you understand? Yes I do but my girlfriend like to go off track and well get notice and I don't like being in this situation, I don't neither, well go and get her. Meanwhile Mark went to search for Jessie and Kelly said we cannot stay with them because they are putting us in danger and I refuse to be in danger because of them, well stop being so paranoid, well I am not but it is true, and then once again they kiss and meanwhile Mark walks off the elevator and then walks through the lobby and step outside and then wander off the opposite direction and went toward the city and looking into store and meanwhile Jessie was laying on the blanket and then suddenly saw the zombie, almost trying to grab her and at that time I somehow I got up and ran for my life.

I didn't know which ways to run but I ran and I got inside the hotel and I didn't know which floor but I went to the higher floor and when got off and somehow I knock at each door and then Kelly open it and said where is Mark? I didn't know that he was looking for me? Where did he when I think he went to find stuff, well I think he is a ass, well no he is not but supplies are good, well if you don't have a weapon and you get caught by zombies that is a totally bad idea, well I will go and find him, well he is on his own, well I am going and you are not stopping me, fine! About one hour the earth shook and what going well it is a small earthquake, well will the earth open up? I don't have the answer for that's but we will be fine. well I need to find Mark, now, okay but we careful like you care.

I do we are friends I thought, well you are wrong. Thanks for being so friendly, well you just rub me the wrong ways, but I cannot explains it but you are being honest, thanks! Mark was still walking in the open and I thought well I will go inside and then I will get more new clothes, then I will get the shoes and I will get the money from the cashier, and about half hour, he took what he wanted but then he notice that he was not alone, and now what I am stuck inside and then I need to gets out in the back door and then somehow Jessie snuck out and search for Mark and Jessie knew what kind places he like to buy and now he just thinking will the back door will help him out from the zombies, but now he was mistaking and meanwhile Jessie was trying not to be spotted by them and them, Jessie called out his name but he didn't hears it and then Mark got out and when into a different direction and headed more into the city, and Mark was aiming toward the bank to steal some loot and think that we help him out but then Jessie was surrounded and try to be silent and but the zombies were smelling her and they were saying we wants your brains and at that moment some how Jessie didn't think but push a few down and then ran back to the hotel and got back to the hotel and saw it was clear and was happy that she was not bitten or hurt, but meanwhile Mark kept on walking and walking into trouble.

Mark kept walking and didn't think where he headed but then he realize that he was in deep shit and didn't know which direction to head Mark when too far and now he is surrounded and there was no escape but he didn't give up, but he just kept walking and then he notice like a hundred zombies chasing him and now he was frighten to death and he notice that he drop the gun on the ways and he knew that he will be dead meat if he does not think fast. Now what I am going to do and I don't know if I am going to make it, and I know if they catch I will be goner and I don't wants that's! Mark was alone and scare and didn't have no device to contact them and Mark was on his own and now he felt that he was in deep shit and couldn't cope with what going on and he knew that he had to go on inside and then go through the building and find the open to get to the hotel but still he was stuck and he didn't know how to get away and he thought probably that Jessie were find him but he waited and waited but no one came and I was alone and they were coming inside and then, I will hide under the bar and they will not sees me but they probably will smell me and they will grab me and I don't know, and now Mark was in fringe panic and he knew that he couldn't stick around there long and then, he heard gun firing and he thought he were probably escape but then he thought he were get shot and because they would think that I was a zombie, but I hope my friend will rescue me, and I was wrong to go out here and how I know and but it is too late, and they are coming in and I need to hide now and not be seen, and they were very close to him and he felt a hand coming toward him then they somehow ran out because someone started fireworks and now he thought I will leave and I will duck between cars and climb the fence and go over and I sees the hotel and I am not too far and

I think that I am going to make it and meanwhile that Kelly and Jeff, and Jessie, said I need to find him, but I wants too. What do means? He could be in danger and the zombies could be eating his brains, yes.

No, I don't wants to listen to this, I just wants to save my friend, you can help him just by staying here and I believe that he will make it back, how can you says that I am going there, go on and I will not stop you and about two hour later somehow Mark got to the hotel and he didn't know how he did it. But then he step into the elevator and then push the button and it went up and then when it got on the floor and he step out and then Jessie came out and said you son of bitch where were you? Well I when and search but then I was trapped and I somehow got away and I make it back and then Jessie when up him and said don't do this again! Okay I won't and you don't wander off to the beach neither, I promise that I will stick with you like glue, good and then Jeff and Kelly said this is not over and but I notice there is a helicopter on the roof and we need to get there, well why don't we go there now? But we cannot because the zombies are up there and we need a distract and I think that we need bait and Kelly said I am not going to be bait, and then Jessie said well I am the fastest runner and so I will do it, and Mark said no you are not and I will volunteer and do it, well I am too, don't argue with me right and don't be stubborn, I am not and I don't wants you to be the bait and you have problem with your leg, is that true, said Kelly, and Kelly said why don't I just looked at it, well no I don't want you too, what are you hiding? Nothing, so was he been bitten, I don't know but what you are saying that your boyfriend could be turning into a zombie, that is not true, bitch.

We need to watch him and if he does we will shoot him in the head, no you are not I will be the one do it to him, and then he shown them the infection leg and Kelly said I need to put some alcoholic and then put rub it and then sees if it was getting better, well it does not hurt and so leave me alone, I will be able to run, trust me, okay it is your life.

That's true but you wants to do it fine, and Jessie went with Jeff and Kelly and now she was really terrified about Mark and but worry he will make it, how do you know, I am just thinking positive and that all I can do right now and then Jeff said we will have aim and shoot and killed those zombies on the roof and but then Mark said to himself what am I doing here if they leave me and the zombies will eat me up and now Mark did not like the position that he was place and he thought that he was a fool to do this and if he died and he were become a zombie.

Huh! Mark scratch his head and then they started to approach me and now I was scare but then when I saw the opening and I just ran inside and shut the door and when up to the roof and I saw them fighting with them and now I knew that I had to step in and then I killed one zombie but it really didn't die and tried to grab my leg and then I saw the blood and I knew it was too late for me and now I need to save my friends so I just jump in and told them get into the helicopter and fly and Jessie said I am not leaving you, and then he said it is too late, and I been bitten I told you that it were been better if I did it but I was wrong and so I just had to do it.

Later that day, Mark said take it up now and don't save me, and Jessie said I am staying with you, no you are not and you wasting time, no I am not going, you stupid bitch, that will not make me go with you calling me names, well I had to but you decided to stay and be dead meat,, you make your choices and I think that you should have gone with Jeff and Kelly, don't you realize that how much I love you, but I need to tell you that I just enjoy having sex with you, you are liar,, but you were great in bed, well that was only a physical relationship, well but it was only a sexual relationship,, you pig and I should gone, but we still could have fun, at a time like this, well life is too short since the epidemic. Yes that true and I cannot be angry with you, come close to me, what wrong with your face, nothing but you are not the same you are a zombie!

ZOMBIE IN LOVE

Jessie came close to him and at that moment he tried to kiss her and Mark lips fell off and then, and Jessie said you are dead? I think that you are right, but I will not hurt you., stay away from me, Jessie said why I didn't listen to you and I stay with you, because you loved me, yes that true come closer to me, I am afraid, you have no reason too. Jessie step near to him and said don't eat me, and I won't bite you, and I promise you, I won't! meanwhile Jeff and Kelly said maybe we should fly back to get Jessie, are you nut and then she will lies that I try to rape her, well let he stay with her boyfriend, okay! That true that tattoo girl deserve what she gets, yes and don't worry Mark will take care of her, yes he will went he become a zombie he will eat her brain, yes so what?

Meanwhile, Jessie was sitting near Mark and then she saw him drooling and then he eyes were getting a bit red and his face was getting pale and he started to make sound instead of speaking and then Jessie said how are you feeling? But he didn't answer,, just make a sound he was not talking to her anymore and now Jessie was scare and now she was wandering how to escape but there was no escape now she was shaking and being very nerve and wanted to leave him but he refuse to let her go! Jessie got up and then Mark grabs her and didn't let her go and then he bite her and she fell and then her bite her head and ate the brain.

The blood was dripping and then he started to rip her apart and then Jessie up and was a zombie, and Mark and Jessie called out for more zombie to comes, and they started to climb and then they were all on the top of the roof and but Jeff decided well maybe we should save her but then he lower the plane and saw that it was too late and she became a zombie and Kelly said if we came here about one hour earlier and she were been alive and now she is a zombie and with Mark and they wanted to reach the helicopter, and said don't let them reach us, they wont. Then Jeff flew over the roof and saw a lot of splatter and blood and body parts on seeing kidney and heart torn apart and Kelly said I have seen enough let leave, yes we are going to Maui, good to hears, and Kelly knew that the chance were slim and didn't says anything to Jeff, and Jeff was very quiet and he knew no place was safe from the zombies.

Kelly sat back and then said where the map that Mark got is and shown you zone free zombies, well what is the location. I don't know but I don't like living in the "world of zombies" and that is awful and I don't wants to is be here, but that was mess up with the contagion and the virus spread, and we had no clue what really happened, well I think it was with the flu shot when wrong, oh you mean the swine flu shot, yep!

About half hour later, Jeff and Kelly landed at Maui and it seems clear.

Do you think so? Yes I think it is safe and I don't see any dead bodies to around and no bloods, well that is a good sign. Hope that you're right, yes you are right and we can just walks freely and then we can walks to the beach, that good. I can breath easy here and I just want to put on a pillow and sleep for days. But are we able to do so? Yes we will be and it is on the map, so this place is no zone zombies that are correct?

I am relief, so am I and he hold her hand and walks and walks until they got to the hotel and walk in and didn't looked around and said now we can rest and nothing to worry about and she smiled and gave him a kiss and then they found a room and open the door and when inside and lock the door and when into separate beds and fell asleep, and but Kelly heard sound from below but she didn't says anything to Jeff.

But Kelly decided to looked around and left Jeff alone in the room and took the key and when out and looked around but it was empty, and she thought her mind was playing with trick on her and then Kelly looked out and so many persons on the beach and she thought they were alive and did not think that they were dead, but the living dead, and decided to go out and didn't know that she was about run into zombies. then decided to turn around and said nope I need to go back and then when back to the room and when to the bed and fell asleep and the next morning the sound and no one was there and then Kelly was going to mention that she heard something but it was her imagination but kept to herself. But then Jeff said where did you go last night? So you were not sleeping no I was not and I just don't like you just wander off and you could be caught by zombies, but you said there are no zombies here. Well I can be wrong and you could been dead meat and they were have comes up and eat me up too, and I am very mad at you for leaving me alone and leaving the door open and I could been taken and you were had to find me but you didn't shown them here, but don't do this again.

I promise that I will stay with you and I will not run off and leave you behind, and then we can looked around and find more weapons and then we can just leave Maui and then we can go to the big island of Hawaii, is that a good suggest, I guess so, but you don't says too much,, I know I don't sorry, I am just a scientist, well but also a good fighter, that is true, I will not denied this at alls, sure you are a smart woman.

Thanks for saying that's but sometime you do get on my wrong side I know so do you, thanks! But I am glad that you didn't abandon me, and so am I. but I won't repeat myself about sometime you can be a bitch and you are a bastard, well no more please, okay just focus and getting the hell out of here, yes I agree with you my "zombie Lover".

What did you says? I called you my zombie lover, no I am not a zombie, and I know well can I just joke around. This kind of joking I don't care for, now you are sounding like a jerk, well around you, I just don't like how you think that you are better than I am. But I don't think that ways, sorry that you feel that ways, okay, I will not call you my zombie lover.

I am not a zombie and if I was then you would have killed me and then you were not have no one to love and so I think we are a good pairs don't you agree and then Jeff said of course I do, and then so we have to fight the battle to win the war that is true, yes it is, so let go and get out of here but we just got here and I just want to go and you know that we are still in some kind of danger, yes I do and I just want to be safe so do I.

Later that evening, Kelly was stare out of the window and she didn't feel conformable able being here, you are right and once again we did lose more friends, that is true but they were really not close friends, because they were bitter and they were out of control and I couldn't stand the tattoo girl she was a really bitch. Not really but they were all right!

But I don't wants to speak about the dead, well just focus and think that we will get out of here. We will get out and we will not get hurt and then we will run to the helicopter and fly out of here, I hope that we can make it, and don't have any doubt, I do and I feel that I been beaten up and threw away but otherwise, but I know that I could deal with it, are you sure? Yes I am but I just don't go out and then you freeze and I won't!

Can I take your word, of course you can think that I am fragile but I am strong and I do have the strength and that is good.

About four later, Jeff and Kelly left the suite and we will need to find the helicopter pad and a helicopter too and we can go to the big island of Hawaii, yes that is the plan, and I hope it works out and but we will not have problem of killing off the zombies one by one, just Jeff before you came along, and I killed them and somehow I knew how to do so.

But don't doubt me and I am solider and I will win and then we will not died or get infection by the virus and so far I do not feel ill , I don't neither.

At this point they were ready to leave and they need a version to distract the zombies and get to the car or go on the top of the building, but Kelly said it were be better if we just go to the car and drive to the airport and you might not agree but I believe it is the right choice but I didn't make it and you did, and you are kind of being bossing and I don't like it Jeff, well too bad and I think that I should make a decision.

Okay! I will go along with you and if we run into any trouble and I won't rub in and I will keep my mouth shut and okay! You are such a nag and you make me sick, Kelly, thanks a lot and I did save your ass so many times, so you don't appreciate me, that not true, yes it is and I don't wants to fight with you and I just wants to beat the zombies so do I.

So you are on the same page, yes I am and so let go now, am I going and don't be slow, I am going my own speed, is that okay with you?

They walks and walks and they saw the red firebird and they both got inside and drove away and they would headed to the airport and find a helicopter and fly to the big island and go there I don't think we should go to Australia, no we need to check the big island and pick up some papaya on the trees and pick and eat, well that sound good, and we need a bag and pick them but we need to gets there first. You are right, I like what you saying and let find the plane fly out from here immediately, but a bit patience, I am but sound like you a bit stress, don't says that's okay! Then Kelly said I dealt with zombies since 2006, and then in 2011 and now, and you think that you know everything but you don't, stop this right, okay but that is true, Kelly. Kelly went the jet at the airport, called out to Jeff and he said not that and then they saw the zombies coming in and we better do something now. Jump in right and locked the door, okay I am but they are banged the door, and saying "I want brains". Do you hear that? Yes I did, Jeff whisper to Kelly, they are going to break in.

Silent to the essence, went they try to get inside pull out the knife, and stick into the head, I am but somehow the door strong and unable to broken was relief and then there was a silent and then the siren. Sirens went off and then you heard gun firing and zombies from the background, I am going to stick out my head if the coast is clear, are you crazy. No, I am not crazy but this opportunity to not being trapped in the jet, but I think that time to get out, fine, I will go along with you, and I am not sure that you are right, so stay in the plane, well find I will looks around, make sure that you take the weapon, of course I am not emptied hand, I am not crazy, okay I don't want to hears that crap, well your p m s acting or your period, none of your business. Kelly step out and shut the door, went I called out and let me in, I will don't worry I won't let the zombies eat you up, promise me, I will let in, fine, Kelly had strap around her waist with bullets and grenades, and walking around behind the planes and spotted the little girl and almost said hey but then Kelly was quiet and snuck between to plane and walks back and was block and didn't wanted to make sound, then I walk backward and then Jeff open the door and ran out and beat up and grab her and pull her inside and you son of bitch and I would have been all right and now they know where we are, now that great it is all your fault, but don't blame me, I am not, yes are, well I don't want talk with you, but why? I am not in the mood and leave me alone. Fine, Kelly just walk in the first of plane did you sees the body at the pilot; well will he become a zombie? Good question, oh I see some movement, I guess but gets ready and now shoot at him.

But we cannot shoot are you a totally idiot? No, I don't like acting jerk.

No, I am not. But just stab him, maybe he is not a zombie, let him speak, fine, then it might be too late, then the pilot got up and his creepy eyes and curve walking, yes he is the pilot so stab is head before he chew your hand off, I am but then Kelly got knock down and Jeff pointed right into the skull and killed the zombie, Kelly was relief, you save me, my hero.

Stop calling me hero, you are some smart ass but with your remark doesn't help the situation, well don't be sarcasm, you are pig now you are calling names, we should be helping each others, yes and not disagree, yes, yes I totally agree, then he came up to him and took his hand and notice that he had a cut, and I need to clean it up and not to get infection, fine but we don't have water to wash it but I will find a medical kit.

Then I rub his hand against her hand and put his hand around her neck and against his body, and you smell so nice, you must be kidding, I really need to take a bath, and change clothes, and have perfume and some make up and hot dress, and high heel, but I am in tee shirt and dirty jean, I must looks bad, no you don't you are hot, babe. But please don't called me babe, I won't! then he kiss her but his cut bleeding, well you need to hold this cloth tight, I will wrap up and Jeff said I want to make passion love to you, but I just be near you, well I like that, he gave her a hug and hold her tight, I like it, but you really want to make love right now, this instant, the kiss and the burst into the jet and try to pull out Jeff with his pant off, and then Kelly said well I will rescue, you, but they ripping me apart, and suddenly Kelly came out with her bra and underwear , and started to shooting one by one then they fell to the ground, and somehow he manage to escape, and lock the door like it was jammed door and then he went to the seat and started up the engine and went to the runway and soon the plane went up and now Kelly said that now we are up air, and then the plane choke and was falling face down what? We will crash, no it won't, and something happen and the plane was level and now Kelly and Jeff sat in the front, and over the ocean, and now they were seeing zombies coming out from the water, I cannot believe it, I do.

The plane went over the pacific ocean and pass diamond head and north shore, and then Kelly said well I thought we would Maui but we were still Oahu, so now we are heading to the big island of Hawaii, well won't we run into the zombies too? I guess so. Kelly was looking at the view and Jeff put on auto pilot. Kelly said did you bring some candy or some waters; nope I left them at the airport, that great! Okay said Kelly but I am starving, so you don't know, but I would some loving from you, but comes close too me. Kelly came close and he grab and Kelly was on the floor of the Jeff rip off her bra and suck her breast, and then she was on top of him, and then the plane was shaking and the wind came and the storm got dark, and the plane was going down and Jeff push her off and fly the plane, thank a lot for leaving me went you got hard on, well we could have crash, and died. Okay, don't panic, Kelly I have everything under control, good to hear Jeff, and Kelly said I will wait until we land at big island. Kelly lie back and fell asleep, and about half hour later they landed and Jeff said sleep head wake up, oh are we here all ready? We had landed, yes we are going to explorer this area and do you think will be safe, I think. Then they both got out and lock the plane and then Jeff said we have a hole in the plane. So what going happen if we are able to go up, I don't want to stick here, I think that we will.

Hope that you are not humor me why should I? I am being honest with you and I just wanted to look around and just get the hell out of here, and end of story, well don't be rude to me. I am trying to explain what we are in and how we will get out of it and then we will be fine, do you trust me? Of course I do and that all it counts that we have trust, I like that's and I will not disappoint you, good, and then we walks in the woods of Hawaii and Kelly said well I think that I can pick some fruits and hope that we will find some supplies, and they when around the area and then Kelly we are not alone here, I think that I hears zombies, I think that you are right, I do like that you agree a lot with me but it is true.

So we need to find a house to hide out and lock and doors and windows and we will be safe, well we are in paradise, but zombies will inference with our fun. Well we didn't comes here for fun and pleasure but we can to get away from the dead and so we didn't and now we might be stuck here and now you are telling me the truth and we are stranded on this island and we will not be able to go to Australia, yes that what I am saying and hope that we will make it alive, now you are pissing me off,, well I don't like your fowl language, well that is to bad, about our circumstance, fine. Kelly said I saw a house beautiful place surrounded by the water, and I think that is a good place, I don't think so. Didn't notice that zombies are coming out of the water and sand and graveyard, yes and now the rain is pouring and now we really have to go inside.

Shown me where that house? Well it is house on the left and I think it is the closer and safe for the night and we will think of the maneuver and I think that we can gets to the plane and fix and fly away. Do you think it work and don't have no doubt, okay I won't and then we will make it, I like positive thinking, so do I, but we need to find mores guns.

If we win the battle and we will win the war and then, we can get far, far way from here, and then we will not be frighten and scare, that is true but when it started I was the strong and I didn't give up but now I think I am having a nerve breakdown. I don't think so, and I just wants to be warm in your arms and be safe from the zombies, so I know but I don't know what tomorrow will bring but now I know that I am with you and you don't have to worry, and I don't wants to be alone, you won't I lost a lot of my friends because of the epidemic and I am not going to get me down, do you understand? Yes I do, and I need to be honest with you Jeff, that once I just wanted to be with someone but when you came along I just wanted to be with you, okay, I do feel the same about you, Kelly.

At that moment they find the house and broke in and then when inside and well it looks like abandon, well those peoples left in the hurried.

TERROR IN PARADISE

Kelly said what happened? Where are those peoples that live in this house, where have they gone? Those are good question, well I don't know but we can stay here for while. Yes but first thing why don't we just locked up and close every doors and windows, and then I will take a shower and get change of clothes and then sleep in this king size bed and those warm cover, but you know comes close to me and I will give you a massage and then I can give you a back rub, that nice and we can have some red wine and talks like real lover, yes that is great! But meanwhile his mind is racing and then said well just rest and let me rub your hand and put your head on my chest, and it is how I like it.

Tell me about you, well I live in Los Angeles and I work in the lab and then I came up with the antidote and then it just went all wrong. I don't understand. Well my antidote for the swine flu somehow got mix up with the plague and then they started to give shot to everyone and they started too died and then come back to live.

Do you sees what happening now, they died and they comes back, yes and it is really awful, I know they are coming over the house, how do you know, looks out, some are standing front of the door, and they want to break and do you have gun and bullets to shoot them that we are able to escape, yeah! I think so, I don't know what you saying, and well right now we don't have a way out. But we cannot stay here neither I know but how, well this has a back door so we will try to see if we are able to sneak out and not be seen and did you sees that boat neck to the dock, yes so from here to there we should go there and get off this island, good idea, I like it. I thought you were so about in half hour we will do that and you follow me, do you understand? Totally I do, and they talked about the plan for a while and make sure that she was on the same page has he was.

But when he got mad, you could tell in his eyes how mean he was, and then Kelly tried to says that maybe they should go the opposite direction and he said no that were be a mistake and that is fine and I will just follow you and that is good and I don't wants us to be separate from each others do you understand? Yes and then it was time to go and sees if Jeff plan were work, and but Kelly had some doubt about his plan but was silent, and then Jeff said what wrong, if we starts running we will maybe not make it, once again you think that I am stupid or dumb but I am not so let me execute this and we will get far from this place,, but Jeff you are repeating yourself, sorry bad habit to be in, when you are trying to make it alive. Yes but are able to get way and not be caught by the zombies? I don't know, but I am willing to try but if we fail we will end of dead, I don't like what you saying but deal with it and it will not go way!

Meanwhile, sat and waited for the right moment to leave, And Kelly was not too happy that she was a bit worry and a little hesitate about the whole situation that will go down soon, but then she said to Jeff, sure I am afraid but I am willing to do it, we went through the drill and you know what you have too do? Yes, I am stupid and I am fighter, I didn't say anything to put you down. That is right but focus and we will get out of this place and we will sail way, I like that's but I think there are too many zombies out there! I think that you are right! But we have no choice but just try to escape this terror and be safe, I do agree with you Jeff, thanks!

Now they were on there ways out of paradise and the zombies were not too far from them, they knew that had to reach the boat and sail from the big island and then Kelly didn't miss the beat and kept up with Jeff and then they got close to the boat but they had to fight to get into the boat and then Kelly said we will make it and I know that we will, yes and don't give up, I wont, and then they killed the few zombies and then they got inside the boat and Jeff took off the rope and then they row out and then Kelly said they are in the water, I know and I don't like this I don't neither.

About half hour they were far from the island and they both were relief and Jeff said I don't know when the wave comes in and the storm and I hope that we don't crash, we won't you don't know, that is true.

They both row and then it was toss up and down and Kelly right now getting sick and Jeff said what wrong? I just cannot be on the water, well you have sea sickness? Yes and I don't this ugh feeling, I know it ca n get you down but I do sees land and Kelly was happy to hears that but they have no clue where they are at this moment. But Kelly looked around and said well are we still in Hawaii? Yes we are and we didn't pass the island, I guess it good, am not sure at this moment and then they got to the island and Kelly said we need to looks around but you know that we cannot go no further right now, well we are staying here, okay! But we might be trapped by zombies but I don't sees any sign of zombies here, I don't neither and we should sleep near the boat, just in case that we need to get away, yes, I agree but if it rain or wind and we are not protection I know, but we have no choice but stay here, yes I know.

But I think this is not such a good idea and we can be seen and that true bit if we go further into the woods we probably get stuck and run for your life and I don't want that again! No! I don't but so we need to be on guard, and then, we can run and be safe, but I saw some movement in the water, you don't say! About a second ago, well they can comes out of the water and drool on us and then we will get infection, I don't like this not all, that true, but watch and sees and what happened and make sure that you run to the boat and no matter what! Yes I know, I heard the drill.

DARK TERRITORY

Suddenly it got dark and Kelly said what going on I don't know.

But then the rain that fell down and the wind and then about hundred zombies, and then they were approaching us and now we had to run and run and then we need to hide and but there are mores coming and then I don't know which ways to run but hide I don't know but Jeff, stay close to me, these are "Thin ICE Zombies, that they are varied type are the worst bunch, they attack and then eat your brain and drain you out and eat your heart and kidney and I don't like this and where are we really, then Kelly looked and said we are at the island of the zombies that the experiment when wrong and they were export here, so how do you know that I was the one that told them and now I don't know when they shipped them here, and how many there are? I don't know the number but it is not good for us, yes I know but we should turn around and head back to the boat and get the hell out of this place, if we get deeper in this dark territory we will not escape, how do you know, I have a bad feeling about this place and I don't wants to stay,, so we need to side track back to the boat. Yes, good idea, Jeff and I am behind you and let head back now and then we can somehow get back and not being seen, good, and also we need some distract and then we won't be trap, yes. But we will survive the night and then the morning, and then we can leave this place, but it could be too late, I don't understand; now it is a risk. What do think that we will be chew up and spite out from the zombies, yes and they are a viscous and they really chew up your brain and they work in group? What, I don't know if understand what you saying don't get caught, I won't, stand by me and I protection you and who will protection me? I will, don't worry we will be fine, I don't think so we need to maneuver from here immediately, and then we can sail away, I like that's and it will happen and then we will go to Australia, and then we will be in safe haven and then we will be happy, and how do know it didn't spread into Australia and I don't but I am not going to stay here and get killed neither, I agree, Jeff and I don't like it here and I have a bad, bad, feeling about this place, okay I do hear you, loud and clear, and they walks side by side and then they reach the boat and they need to fight with the zombies and then they got inside the boat and then a little girl, zombie sat in the boat and Kelly said what should I do? Well, if she approach you, killed her, and then the little girl came closer and was about to bite me, and I threw her overboard and we were safe once away and then we sail for day and days and we thirsty and hungry and we didn't sees land for days and we were burn by the sun and our skin were ugly and stinky and when we got deeper and deeper in the ocean and the darker it got!

At that moment for some stupid reason I got up and stood up on the boat and Jeff said are you crazy and the boat almost tip and we almost feel into the water and now we both were terrified, but at that moment we were fine and we were safe. I thought and then they ram into us and we had no place to run but I somehow manage to sneak out and I now I was freed and I needed to safe Jeff and I don't wanted to be alone so I fight until I got Jeff, and we somehow we end up on this island and we need to not to stay but then Jeff said I saw some fruit trees with papaya, and I pick up a few and I couldn't carried a lot, and Jeff helped me out and I didn't like that we were going sleep in the tenth and then someone had to watched the night and I volunteer and then Jeff refuse to let me do it but I still not I had the experience, and then he said okay!

Later that night, somehow I just doze off and suddenly Jeff woke me up and said you are watching out for our interest, and Kelly to refuse that he was right and I was not a good solider at that time, and Jeff took over and we will be ready to kills them, and then Kelly agree that she was too exhaust and had a pain and then Jeff said I will get us out and then fine, I won't stand for it and now I will looks for wood to burn and keep us warm.

" Then Jeff said I keep watch and you take a nap and I will tell you when I sees some activity, and we will just try to take off, but the boat had some damage and Jeff said I will somehow to fix it and then we can sail away.

Kelly was sleeping and then she had a bad nightmare and woke up pointed the gun toward Jeff and he said what are you doing? Well I thought they were coming near us and I was ready to shoot but you almost shot me,, and don't get out of control., I won't but I will save you and I know that you will do the same. Yes I would and so Jeff and Kelly hug and but he was frighten but he refuse what was really happening and he was just silent but Kelly knew that Jeff was keeping secrets from her, and Jeff knew that they were have to leave in the early morning! But Jeff said I will keep the firing going and but don't worry we won't be seen and then Jeff mention that we can cross the river, and Kelly said what river? But then Kelly said well I didn't see the river and where is it location? I will show you in the morning, good and she fell asleep.

About one hour later, Jeff woke up Kelly and said it is time to wakeup and what going on and the zombies are on there ways here! No, I cannot believe it, but don't you see them coming? Yes they are coming very close and I don't like it, I don't neither, well that is really bad, yes it worst they spotted us, yes they did and they are really fast those Ice zombies, and then they will aim right to our brain, no kidding but we will survive this yes, what a ordeal, that we are going through, yep!

We need to cross the river but we will still be stuck on this island that is true.

But then we will found another boat, and sail away and then we can sail far way from here, I am not too happy at this point, I am not.

So Jeff and Kelly started headed to the river and then Jeff said well we have to walks about two miles mores, I cannot walks I am really weak. but you must, and you don't want to be eaten up do you? No I don't!

THE RED RIVER

Jeff and Kelly walk the two miles and then they approach the river and then Jeff said, and said looks at the water. It is red river and said, and I don't want to go into that water, and then Jeff hold my hand and I was afraid that I would slip and fall into the water, but I didn't and Jeff hold me tight. Jeff didn't let me go and then I was holding on and I was so scare and afraid but I didn't say to Jeff and I knew that he somehow that I was afraid and then I just follows him and I walks very slowly and I across over and so did Jeff. That night we stop for the day ands he continues walking and walking the woods got darker and then we just stop and stay for the night! Jeff put the blanket on the ground and told me to sit down and I did, then we cuddle together and we got warm and but it felt cold but it was the night of Hawaii and but I was surprise with the chill. And then they started to hear sound and groaning and moaning and I now I was really scare but I had the gun in my hand and then I was really to shoot. But I kept one eye open. But I still awake and I knew that we could here for a little while and then we had to leave the area soon. When the sun came up it was time to get out of here, do we have too? Yes they will come and gets us, well I don't like that but fine I will put on my shoes.

Then she saw a s snake coming close and it looked like it was infection with the virus and don't get bitten by the snake and you probably were turn into zombie, well I don't like it,, and so we will hike for more miles and then we will find a car but we will not be able to drive across the ocean but we will need to figure out how we will do the escape from this location, and don't worry your head and we will find a ways.

" They are coming hurried we cannot stall for time, no we will not so don't panic" I am not but I know that we need to go now but it is still dark out there and it will be a problem but it will be more of problem if we stay, that is true, well we just keep moving and don't let them smell you and they are more progress and they are the undead, I know and you don't have to reminder me,, I was you know what our trouble are. I know them and you don't need to tells me I know but now you are acting like a bitch, thanks a lot but I also wants to save our lives, everything you says that is true and so I won't argue with you and I will just listen and paid attention and hope that I won't get mess up what you are saying, listen I been situation before and I think that we will be fine, well you are not insure about it and I don't trust your judge me okay! But don't be so sacrum, and you acting like that you know everything, but I don't but I do not know how to fight them and how to stop them, Sure I do too.

Kelly said follow my steps and do you sees the river flowing quickly and I don't sees those faces from the river and they are definite but I still not sure where directions but we need to go west and down that bridge and heading south, and think that I saw a few boats there! Hope that you are right? I am doing have doubt, Jeff was started to getting a little mean and then said I will be taking over this, fine. Yes you will not do thing different then I am? Well, maybe I will. Now Jeff and Kelly were started to argue and Kelly said " stop this instantly" what you are going beat my ass, now you are sounding like that you know everything but you don't and I am not saying that I do! But I do have the experience fighting with the zombies and so do me and don't say that I don't. Well I am not and don't put word in my mouth, okay! About five hours later, Jeff and Kelly notice a cabin and then, Jeff said well now we have a place to stay, yes we do. And we need to rest too, yes and then we will looks for a helicopter to find and get away, yes, yes and now we will go inside and then we can put on the fireplace and then we can be warm but Hawaii is not cold, and it is a warm climate, yes I know and I believe that maybe someone will find us,, yes that were be good. But now we need to swim in this water to get across and then we will walks on the other side and then we will find a boat and maybe a helicopter that we can fly away from and I cannot wait to get out of and I am so frighten and scare and I just want to go back home, but then Jeff said we cannot go back home because it is in battle with the zombies and you will died there and the risk it too high so we will be going to Australia and we will be fine, but you said we were be fine here and we are not! Don't be so angry at me, I am just trying to save ours lives and you are just dragging your feet and I think that you are pathetic, that is such a low blow and you are not better and defending with zombies., and you are helpless, no I am not I did survive the war with them but the battle is going on and I don't know it will end.

But now we need to move, so I am ready and I have pack back and I am ready to go, but hope it is not too heavy, no it is not! But don't worry about your worry your head about it and it my stuff and I will be responsible for it and you just gets us out of here, fine that what I am trying to do, and so I think crossing the red river and we will be near that house and it might have some kind of transportation to leave this misery island of the dead, I agree and I just don't like it here, but you are such a winery, well maybe I am but I still make it without you, thanks a lot of my support.

Well I am doing my best and we don't have a lot of weapon and we just have enough to make too tomorrow, that dim news to tell me and well I need to keep you inform of the situation that we got us into and us and I am just wanted to leave but there but only dead end and stuck between the river and civilization, yeah! But did see that just ran by? Now I think that you are seeing things and I think that you might be sick, no way am I not sick and you trying to trick me, no I am not and stop saying that. Jeff. Okay! Jeff said to Kelly I am going first to walks the rock and get to the other side, and Kelly said I am coming too, but listen and wait until I cross, you are going to leave me and I refuse to stay by myself. Fine, don't be so stubborn, I am not you need me, yes like a hole in the head. I feel that you putting me down and so go by yourself and I will wait for you being such ass. Later that day Jeff cross over and walks around and meanwhile Kelly sat down and looked around and was calm and Jeff kept going further and further into the woods and then Kelly didn't sees him and started to get worry but still stay on this side. Wait and wait and no sign now Kelly was about to cross over and but then Jeff came back and said I didn't found anything that on that side so Jeff came across and then something came out of the water and Kelly was getting worry and Kelly jump in and she pull Jeff and said " are you okay" ? He shook his head and said yes, but felt like something bite,, and now Kelly hold her head and said, yes I sees the bleeding, and said sorry Jeff it is the virus, and how do you know, you have the sign and the bite marks, and I don't know how long will it takes, but you will died, please don't tell me that I don't wants to hears negative stuff from you, well it is really serious and you will died tonight and I will have to shoot you, are sure? Yes I am, what have you done? Well I try to off this island and now I will died on this island, go figure, well maybe the immune will save you and it could be fifty chance that it will, thanks a lot, then Kelly put some alcoholic on it and rub on the wound and sat and cry and then Jeff said why are you crying, well I loss a lot of friends of this epidemic, and I don't wants to lose you neither. But I need to be ready to killed you, you are not a killer, I know and but you will become a zombie and I have no choice, yes you do? What? Test me first, what I don't understand, if the blood check out to be clear and not infection,, yes but I don't have my test tube but still try for me, okay I will.

Later that Kelly had a gun pointed at him all nigh long and didn't sleep a wink and saw the progress aggressive and it was going to happen any second from now. Kelly felt froze and then felt hurt and then it was happening and the gun when off and Kelly slip and fell into the cave and Jeff had a bullet in his head, and five hours later Kelly woke up and daze and got up and she was weak and then she saw bats flying over her head and now she was afraid that she were get bitten by the bats.

Kelly got up and kept walking through the cave and at the end of the cave Kelly saw an opening and walks out and she smiles and saw a boat on the sand and Kelly walks toward the boat and didn't even think that zombies were in back of her, but kept walking until she reach the boat and push into the water but it was stuck in the sand and she really try to push it but somehow she got the boat into the water and jump inside and about five minute later, Kelly saw zombies on the sand of Hawaii and Kelly was in the ocean drifting and drifting and the waves were really strong but she just hold on tight and then Kelly was far, far way from the island, now Kelly was in the middle of the ocean and about two hours Kelly was surrounded by white sharks and she thought they were attack and then Kelly kept quiet and they were gone and it was one day and then a week and the night were cold and the sun burn her skin, and still in the ocean.

OPEN WATER

Kelly was still drifting and no land at sight. Kelly was starving and thirsty and now started to image things that are not really, at that moment Kelly think that she sees a land ahead but then she slip into sleep and not wake up next morning surrounded by water and no land and now Kelly is freaking out and does not where she is and no contact with anyone and just in the ocean and drifting and drifting away from land, and Kelly most of the time slept and didn't wake up, Kelly was getting really weak and no energy at alls, and just slept and didn't wake up. It was day that became weeks and months, and Kelly was in a tiny boat, and one night the storm came in and Kelly was really weak but somehow to manage to stay in the boat and the boat was tipping into the ocean and Kelly was in a panicked and but most of the time Kelly was out cold and fragile and Kelly thought to herself, will I make it alive. But that night somehow Kelly try to stay wake but barely alive at this time and Kelly didn't know what day it was and what her name, and how Kelly is confuse and dazes and had a lot predators in the water, beside sharks and whales and even some zombies, that she were not able to fight off but one point not give up of living and Kelly knew that there is chance that she will make it.

But suddenly it got pitch black and the rain fell and Kelly had no cover and Kelly got soak wet and was shaking and chill and Kelly losing her mind at this point and Kelly didn't know that if the zombies follows her, or she was just her mind was playing trick at this time, Kelly didn't know and just fell sleep in the pouring rain and Kelly it was a deep sleep and woke up like three days later, and then now Kelly was seeing land and but was not sure, and but still drying up and then once again the rain came and then

Kelly started to cry. Kelly said, please god I didn't do any harm and I am out here and lost in the ocean, please save me, I cannot died here.

Then slept again and wind blowing and the boat was tipping and almost got toss off the boat but Kelly hold tight when she woke suddenly.

Once again was surround by the white shark at this time they were not leave her and now she thought that they were attack her and then but please I don't want to died, and then somehow they left in the suddenly and then Kelly was relief and but still thirsty and hungry and then said maybe I will died in the ocean and not being bitten by zombie and I still don't like this scenario, and I need to sees land, but nothing, and still stuck and the waves were getting higher than the boat.

At that moment Kelly notice a leak in the boat and now what? What will I do? Now, and I will fall into the ocean and drown and get eaten by sharks, and know one will that' I will died at sea and there will be trace of me, no I am not going to give up and Kelly notice that she saw in the boat some kind of rubber that she can keep the water out, and won't sink in the ocean and now she work very hard to keep it tight and close. Now it was seal and somehow Kelly was feeling a bit better, but had a case of sea sickness and was refuse to let her down. But kept on rowing and rowing and but it was too hard and her hands were started to hurt and so she just let the boat to float, and Kelly now started to sees some land and Kelly was happy but she was hoping it were not be the big island of Hawaii that where she escape from and was not planning to go back to that awful island of zombies, so she kept on sailing way further, and further away. but it seem like Kelly was on the sea for more than a month and no coast guard or anyone to sees her and rescue her and now Kelly thought., that she had to find land and then she realize that she had compass, and but was not sure if working but she still took out and looked up to the sun and then she took the boat row and heading west and east and now she seem like it was familiar area that what she thought and then Kelly knew that it was time to write a letter and Kelly find some paper and pen in the medial kit and started to write and how day and if someone find her and she is dead, to tell her family and then after the letter, she put into the medical kit and shut it tight and next to her and lay back and slept and days and days, and then the wave almost blew her off and the boat and Kelly was unhappy that her strength was getting weaker and but not having energy to survive this ordeal, but still staying positive. The wind, the rain, and the sharks came around and they were very near her and thought they were bite her hand off and then somehow Kelly pull out her hand and looks and it was fine and thought I fell asleep and I somehow put on hand in the water, I must be stupid, and I need to be alert and be ready to fight off the sharks otherwise I will be dead meat for the sharks, no ways, I will be on my toes and I will stay awake and I will died and I refuse to do so. Now Kelly was talking to herself and now thinking well I must be crazy and maybe I did the wrong by killing Jeff, but I knew that he were be a zombie and I don't know what going to happen with me but I hope that I get save by someone and I hate being alone in the water and be hunted by predators.

"so the wind calm down and Kelly somehow caught a small fish and ate it raw and then somehow took a little salt water and then spite out and it was really awful tasting and but I need not to the water and the food to make it and now Kelly was like eating raw fish but being caution from the sharks and bigger predators out in the ocean.

At this moment, Kelly was about to take out the fish and then a whale hit her boat and fell out and then swim back to the boat and got in somehow and now she just lay on the bottom of the boat and didn't wanted to be seen by the whale, and about half hour she was alone, and safe and was relief and then she lay low for hours and hours and until the morning sun came in and then she got really a bad burn and Kelly lips were ugly looking and peeling, and white skin that she remove from her lips and started to bleed and I need to stop that now. Is this the end?

RESCUING KELLY AT SEA

Five hours later, Kelly was deep sleeps and the coast guard notice a boat was drifting and then they said we need to looks on that boat and the captain said well Tony, do you think that is a good idea? Yes, but be ready to shoot if come out to be a zombie on board that boat. Sure I did some of this task in the past and I think that the boat might be empty, but not get off track, fine I will not. About five minute later, they found Kelly lying on the boat and she is half dead and I am trying to wake her up, about a minute later, Tony was doing CPR on her and then she woke up and they took her on the coast guard ship and took her to LA and days that she spend in the hospital and but at a private base, and they were taking blood test and sees if she was infection but in two weeks she was release and asked what happened to her, at that time of life she forgot that she was at sea, and moment she forgot her name.

But then she thanks Tony and the crew for saving her life and they told her that there is martial law and she is not able to leave this place, and they asked where you were going? Kelly replies I would go home; well everyone is dead or zombies. Oh! I see. But Kelly didn't like be lock up and not able to go outside and she wanted to help with the epidemic, but they refuse to let her go the lab that is quarantine, at this time. But Kelly kept on fighting and they said well it is your own risk and but the president said it is no one is allowance to leave this place until it is secure and safe and right now there are thousand of zombies out there, do you hears what I am saying., yes I do but I need to help and find a cure, but if you step out you will be shot, well how can I help well there is a lab near the morgue, thanks and I check it out if it suited for my kind of testing, fine.

But it might work but I will check out and Kelly when down to the lab and started to step inside and it looked clear and walks inside and started to take the blood from the dead, that might turned into zombies. but still pinch there finger and put into the test tube and a little sample on a glass and looked through and the cells were like jumping around and now Kelly knew that they will come alive and now Kelly had her gun ready and one of the soldier try to take it from her and she knock him and locked the door and blast the zombies away, and that was not your duty but I still save your life, well you can be court martial because I killed them they were dead all ready. But you need to follow order here, well I am not in the service, I am private citizen, well that doesn't make the different but still you broke the rule and you will get punish and you must be kidding, well that is not fair and justice, because I am scientist and you are trying to stop me killing the zombies that they might kills us alls that is unfair, but I am also helping to find a cure and so just leave me alone, I am busy and I am working on the antidote, and then I will save more lives, I got it and so bug off, well I will tell my captain what you have done, well that was already dead, but next time I will not save your ass, and he walks out and slam the door, and Kelly started to take more blood test.

First subject, sign of cuts and black and blue mark and sign of setting of the infection kicking in and the second subject bite mark on the neck and bruises, and sign of the infection, more extreme stages, in five minutes from now. Well now Kelly got her weapon ready and was about to shoot but didn't stand up and then notice was shot in the head and was really dead, and Kelly was relief and kept on testing and then someone knock at the door and Kelly was about to open but it was a zombie and had bloody teeth and mouth dripping from his mouth that was the soldier, that was going to report me, and I kept the door shut and put on the double seal and I felt safe at that moment and then I heard gun shooting and then a minute later he was dead and I was save once again, and I just kept working and not being distract by anyone, and i work and work but I didn't have the right equipment to work and the right chemical to use. And I thought that I were fail at this time but I still kept testing and until I got results, and then I thought probably I should try on the one that was dead and sees what happened, but I didn't give up until I got it correct. About one hour, I went upstairs and told the general I was ready to go field work and test out on zombies, and the general said you are not allow to leave this place, but I need too. But right now you are going stay in the lab and Kelly was furious and slam the door and walk into the lab and then thought to herself and I have a plan and know one will know that I left, so Kelly thought well I will go to the "service elevator" and I will sneak out that is brilliant, and Kelly was happy about the plan, and not being coop up in the lab and seeing dead zombies but saving lives.

Kelly snuck out and went outside and the soldiers spotted on the sidewalk and she had escape, well we cannot help went she gets in trouble sir, can I just there and watched her, you will take my command and you will still put under my order and she will need our help, she didn't follow order and she is on her own, but Ken didn't like what his general said and he when out for her and the general said that when we catch up with him he will get court martial and he will be in the federal prison, well he is trying to help Kelly and I think I should help Ken, no if you do, you will end up dead.

Ken was on Kelly track and meanwhile Tony snuck out and the general and was left alone with two not that experience men to protection him and then about few minute that were hearing " we wants brains" and he said is anyone watching the door? But we are not sure, Sir. Who was suppose to be doing this, Tony and Ken and they left, well they went "AWOL" yes after that person Kelly, well Tony went to help Ken, same thing don't you think? Yes sir, and go back to your post, they will break in and I don't have enough bullet to killed them. Well use a stick and head them over there head, think men! We are but I don't this situation, I don't neither, and they said well we will guard you sir.

UNDER SIEGE

The battle started inside the hospital and they were trying to killed off the zombies and but they were unable to keeps shooting and missing the target and the General got up and said I will shown you how to killed that zombies, well sir, we are the best shooter but we are not aiming because they are a bit quick. But just kept on shooting and aim for the head and right into the brain, we are but they are still getting up, but you must have missed, no sir but I am shooting them but they fall and then they come back up, well stupid man, you are not hitting them and missing them, let me shown you how to killed a zombie, and the general didn't miss one zombies and but the blood somehow splatter into his mouth and then he stood for a while and fell to the ground and the solider check him out and wanted to do CPR and one of the solider said, don't do it, and the other one said why not? You will get infection, no I won't don't be a smart ass right now we have a opportunity to shoot him and leave this terrible place and I don't wants to hear that's. Fine, and they cover him and then shot him in the head and one of them said you are a killer.

No, I am not and I am just trying to figure out where you stand with the military and but you know that I had no choice and but I still alive. But we have time about when the solar flares comes in and I don't know what you are saying but we need to take cover and we safe but that will activation the zombies and we will have no control and then we will get killed, no we won't. Ken and Tony stand side by side with Kelly and they alls had weapons and aim and shoot and the antidote will not work so it is too late, and that is for sure, and you don't have agree with me but it is true and I just wants to get the hell out this place now, got it miss. Ten four, so you will be talking military talks to me, well I don't understand it. Just keep on walking and don't get any attention and we will be fine, that good, I guess, said Kelly. Now we need to be very quiet and walks very slowly, okay and we can do that's I am glad to hear that, but we are not out of the woods, the solar lights will be flares up and it going to be bright and we will be seen and I don't like this situation I don't neither, Kelly and Tony and Ken, so let move it now, quickly, but I said not make any sound don't you get it, yes I don't want to be dead meat, fine I don't neither . About half later, they were out of the town and the lights started to shine and Kelly said come on now they will sees us and we need hide in the woods, and I don't think so said Tony, with the snakes and the bears, I think the bears and dead and into parts that the zombies ate them, and now do you know? I just know with the things that I sees and sees that they are gone and now they are just hunting for us for brain, so are so envy, no but I think that zombies just wants to eat.

That what you can up with no but I did some test on a few and then it was clear that once they were us and then they were monster.

What I don't understand what you are saying and it a lot non sense, well you should believe what I am saying it is not true and my family is still alive.

But they said the solar flare, and it will be a lot fires, how do you know? But heard it going on sound it will be dangerous and not able to walk out but will we be safe inside, I don't know, but being safe at that moment I don't know, but don't worry, and I will be on your side, Tony, and Ken said you can count on you, I don't know what to believe but I am fine, well we will deal with disaster and we might not survive and being stomped by this ordeal probably, the fire will kill us and the zombies will venous us, I don't want to listens to that. Kelly did refuse what Tony was saying it is the end of world, stopping saying that's! Tony and Ken argument over Kelly, well you have crush for her, and you must be jealousy, no I am not, said Ken.

Ken is that true, said Kelly well you are not my type, and I don't have time to have relationship, right, so now I just to get the antidote. It will time but I don't know the "Solar" comes and I don't know if we are going to make it. Don't be negative, but I am just telling you the truth, face it, I cannot, what I don't understand but be clear, there must be way out. I don't see it now but you will, okay if you say so! Well I do, so if we out we will burn if go inside, I don't know what going happen to us. Believe me we will be fine, don't say it if you don't believe, but then Kelly went into the room and check out the paper and some chemical on hand and mix with alcoholic and water but it is not effective but not giving up, go girl!

Tony got up and said Kelly after this epidemic, will date me, I don't know but I cannot answers it now, I don't what going to happen, just patience and right now, just leave me alone, fine and Tony walk out and Kelly said don't go out too far. I won't, and stop out and took a walk out and then something fell off the building. But it was a close called. Come back in do gets it, don't be ass, and Kelly said right now, don't get me stress out, fine about five minutes the zombies were coming closer and shut the door behind him. Kelly pulled him and double locks the door, one of zombie foot got caught, and Kelly pushes the foot out of door, and did get bitten?

No, I don't know, Kelly checking him out and you look fine, thanks. Ken why did you step out and put us in danger, I need some fresh air and now we have to fight off the zombies, well they would come or not.

Ken they are breaking the windows they are getting through, and sees the drool on the floor, don't get the spite on you and it will effective you and you might the virus, well it might be too late, what do you mean? Not sure but I think I got a bit and I think it will be getting sick, I don't like this and why didn't you tell me. Sorry I was distracted with the solar flares and just don't realized it, fine but you need to be contain from us, why? Don't need to explain it alls over again? Yes I do and it is knowledge not to get sick by a zombie, that very deadly, so then I need to shoot you in the head, well I don't like that scenario, I don't neither.

The fires started and the zombies were getting stronger.

SOLAR FLARES

Do you see what happening in the sky and it will be worst when it hit the earth, I know it will be the end of the world, stop saying that, but it is true.

Kelly walks and said we need to find a place that is safe from fires and from foolproof from that's, I don't understand what you are saying, well we need to be on our guard, we are but our friend got some spite and some he might become a zombies and it could be a slim chance, at this point and why did you scare me so much, well you are careless.

Well you don't have to point it out, and don't do stupid stuff that you did and that our lives are danger, yes I got the point, gets off my case, well, looked the flares are falling and the it burning alls around and I know and we are trapped inside that is awful what should we do? Stand still and I don't think so well I think we have to run and find some other location, your are damn right! Now you are agree with me when you put us in danger I didn't know that I would be the blame, well you are.

Later that day, Kelly said follow me, so where are we going, I believe go underground will be safe, you must be kidding there are a whole bunch of zombies to attack us and now you wants to go back so you wants to be burn like a crisp, well what choice do we have? Done your right so let go now and we will not be torch by the fire. I will be relief when the flares are gone and I don't know how long they will last but I am not waiting here, I am not Tony, and ken. But hurried we need to close the sewer top now, it is wet and dirty and I sees a lot of rats there, I know and they can be zombies rats, I wish that you didn't says that, well sorry but face the truth.

No, I don't wants too but you need too, I am going to keep us save, well also you are controlling us, but I am helping out and you are still

114

complaining, sorry, I didn't wanted to be rude and means but you just get me angry, well you are a bossy and I don't take order but I do wants to survive this so I will listens, good I like that's! Thanks keep on walking and keep your flashlight near you and not to step on something that might alert the undead, good advice, I think so, said Ken.

Later that day! They walks and walks more than a five miles and they hit the dead end and Kelly said we probably end up dead, has I speak because I don't know which ways to go back, don't says that's! Don't panic, Tony, we will work it out and I know that you have a some kind of fear and it small places, well yes you are right! I know but don't be. Kelly went ahead and passes the guys out and looked around each corner of her eye and spotted that zombies were approaching us, so hide, but where? Just hide in the corner and let them pass us and hope that they won't smell us, I know but we will be okay! Be quiet it is very important at this time, they are coming and I don't wants to be there meal, and I don't wants to die, I know silent, they were so quiet and the zombies didn't sees them or smell them and then Kelly said, Tony, don't move. I won't.

Then they heard the explosion and the it was making a lot sound and Ken step out and one of the zombie grab him and Kelly started to shoot the gun and miss the zombies than there were thousand,, oh my god what going on here? They know that we are here, I know and we need to keep on moving, but be careful, I am but somehow from the underneath one zombie pull his pant and he was slipping to unknown origin and Kelly said hold on, do you hear me? Yes I do but help me, I will be torn into pieces and I don't wants to die, I am doing my best, I know but we will save you.

Kelly pull out the rope and tied it and then threw toward him and said catch it, I will try, hurried, I don't know if I could hold on any longer, you will and once again, Kelly threw it and somehow he caught it, and he was pull up but his pant were rip. So what exactly what happen, I just got pulls and I fell down to the hole, and so far I don't sees any marks on the body.

Do you know the meteors shower will becoming soon and we will be more in danger and it will sparks earthquake and tidal waves, that comes and swept off into the water, and the zombies will be in the water and they can catch us and we will be bait, it not going happened, how do you know, I don't, well seem like, we will end dead, looks at the sky it is changes color, seem like it going happen any second, no I don't believe it, watch do sees the movement, I don't but they are here, who?

Zombies, oh no! They ice zombies, and vampire/ zombies walking our ways and they are really hungry, they are really cannibals and eating the eye ball and the brain, that is gross, and I don't die that way, I don't. Kelly stood up, and pulls out the gun and shooting at them

But they are very fast and then Kelly kill one by one and Ken and Tony said well, we are not that strong like you, comes help me out and then they saw them trying to break in and then the fire came and then acid rain and it just grew numbers, and but we didn't stop Kelly but we still killing them and then I thought well maybe I should use the leftover spray and Ken said are you crazy and then your going outside and what? Well I will aim and shoot, you are going to died, no I am not, well you are putting us in danger, and I thought I had too but then I knew it was too much and I ran back inside and slam the door and put some wood and we will be safe and then Kelly said I am the only one that is shooting them.

But Tony was not well and Kelly knew that he was a effect with the virus, and then I will become a zombie and we need the diversion, and you will be the bait but I do volunteer, because you are feeling ill, yes and I think you too just can run and be safe, but we need to stick together to survive. I agree, but Kelly come on Tony I don't wants you to died but you guy I am helping you out and I wants to make it alive just go, we cannot, you are wasting time, no we just want our friend to be with us, so what wrong with that, nothing but don't paid attention, just go. And I will be fine, no you are not! Kelly said well Tony, I just want to stay here, and just go, okay!

METEOR SHOWERS

Kelly said hurried Ken that we need to go now any second the meteor will becoming and then we will be safe toward the mountain and found the cave and stay under, are sure, yes I am but I don't think that I have doubt, but I think I was right about the area to go but this is too much of mayhem and death and I just don't like the skies and they will fall on us don't you get it? Yes I do. But I am not going happen I am just keeps on moving and we will be fine and I know but we will not burn up and into crisp, no we will not just keep low and not to be in the fire of the meteor and I got it and you do the same, said Kelly that is too bad that Tony had to sacrifice and we had no choice and he did get infection and he wanted to save us and so he did and now we are leaving this place and then we will be safe in the mountain and clear air and not in the pollute city and hope not to run into the zombies, but if the virus spread we will run into them and we will just have to win and not lose the battle and I don't see anymore military around they must been killed in the battle by the zombies, I think that you are right and I am thinking anything, but staying alive, I totally agree, with you, and I don't like it. But we just got to get to the cabin by the lake and we can fish and walks freely from the disaster of destruction and I just want you think that we will make it out of alive. So do I say Ken but time is on our side and I don't see any meteor coming toward the earth. But if one hit the earth and it will burn the surface of the earth and the earth will open up and then we will fall in and we will died, well you are really a scientist, yes I am and I really didn't believe you but I am, well that is great, but you hot scientist and I would never guess, but now I know you are a smart lady. Thank you very much and you very kind but we don't have the time to chit chat and so let move on and I worry about you, I can take care of you, I know I can take care of you too, so just walks and stop talking so, fine, now you are being bossy and rude and I don't like it well do you wants to be alive? Yes I do, shut up and move and we will get there much quicker, got it.

About a minute later, Kelly spotted the meteor coming closer and Kelly said snuck down and don't move and the firing meteor miss them by a inch and Kelly said well that was a close called, yes it was and the grass was burning and let move away now, I think it not stop and then the second one was coming and it hit the car and burst into flame and Kelly said we are lucky that we left the car, sure I know we could have been burn to not recognized us, that true but who were be looking for us, the one that love us, if they are alive, hope that they are but not sure at this point, I know but if make me very sad to think about it but I don't wants to talks about family, okay!

Later that day! They reach the cabin and they walks in and it looks like no one live there for month and spider web on the walls and snake crawling on the floor and Kelly said don't worry it is not poison, and Ken said good to hear about that's, and Kelly looked around well the supply are very ancient and we need to go out later to found foods and water, otherwise we will starve, that is true, and more ,meteor were falling and Kelly was worry but didn't wants to scare Ken but kept quiet and then he said well tell me what going on? Well do you want the good news or bad news first, just speak girl, I can take it. But you are fragile no I am not stop thinking that Kelly, I am not I refuse that's! keep on walking and I will not be far from you, do you hear what I am saying I will be fine and I will not be eapture by zombies and not the meteor will not hit me, take my word, I know but it is still like a war going on alls side I know but there is no stop to it and I know just walks and we will be fine, you are confidence in yourself.

Well, if you want to survive this ordeal you need to keep your head up and don't let anything let you down if this the end but you still fight to stay alive, that but I don't know but I am not willing to give up but those meteors are hitting the surface of the earth and the strength being strong and not weak and not able to walk and being caught by zombies,, that we were be very bad situation and I think we should just walks and not talk the possibility of chance, that I don't know but I am just not listening what you are saying and I will be better and I don't wants to know right now but I just wants to get to our destination and that all I care right now, so do you know where that is? Right now I don't know and we will be in the line of fire, no matter where we are. I do hear what you saying but I don't like being here, do you think that I do? No, so be quiet and if I was rude and means I were said shut up but I am not.

Later that day we walks on the side of the mountain and Kelly said I sees the lake and maybe we can cross over and then we can be somewhere else, and then Kelly said we still be where the meteors will still falling from sky and we are middle of the mountain at that moment I thought I was going to fall and then Ken somehow he gave me his hand and I hold it and I thought I was going to let go and I was fear that I were died but then I saw his face and I was on solid ground and then I was relief and then I said I will not go to the edge of the mountain and it is very dangerous and I sees them coming? Who the zombies? don't you sees them, yes I do and we need to run and hide this instantly, got it and I am in back of you, and then later that day they reach the other side and it seem to be clear and no meteors and zombies and right now we can start a campsite, you must be kidding, no I am not and gets some woods and I will set up the tent and we will be fine, okay! I think this is not the brighten idea but it is stupid and risking, well it might be but we are moving until daylight, got it, and you really think that I will be able to sleep, and Kelly said well I will take watch tonight and you can sleep, well maybe I should, no I am and go to sleep and I will keep the fire burning, fine, and Kelly watched all night long and didn't doze off that night.

CAMPSITE

"The sun came out and Kelly sat in front of the fire and thought to herself and looks around the camp fire and it was time to wake up Ken and then he woke up and said what going on and Kelly said well we are going stay here and we are not leaving the woods yet! But Ken is you sure? I know I make the right decision and I think this area is safe, and I don't sees any sign of the meteor and no sign of zombies so we stay put here, if things changes then we will move, is that a bit risking and then Kelly said by going out there is more risking and suicide than here, well I like it here. Ands we are not in the open, and we are hidden in the woods, you are right about that's but I do hears voicing, no,, I don't what do you means that you don't, am I losing my mind, no but the fear is, thanks.

I don't know what to do and I am just afraid that we are going to died, but we are not and you panicked to quick, so calm down and I will hold you but don't sees the sky seems like they are going to break and the water will pour and we will float away, and no we are not! Your imagine is going wild and it not going to happen, well you don't control the weather and we are on soft ground, well we are still solid and don't freak out and it make thing worst, what could be worst than we are invaded by zombies and the world is ending, and it is destruction and scary like hell, I am here and I sees it too, and I am not blind. Then the storm hit and it was very shaking and it started to have mudslide and the ground was wet and it was a lot of mud and Kelly said now we need to go and Ken said but why because it going to give out and we will end up in the river with zombies, well I don't wants that's the world is changing and I don't like the temperature is changing to freeze, no it is not possibly, but it is, I am not disagree, but we still can stay? No, now we are going and we will be swamp and now,

120

fine so unhook the tent and we will be going to west of here, and then we will find a good place to stay, and then the mudslide started and it was not stopping and Ken said, okay I take your word and I am not staying, good hurried up I don't want to be swept away from here, well you such a bitch and I don't take order I give them, well that all I hears from you, and I do need to focus and looks at my compass and which direction, because I don't wants to walks into it but walks away from it, so I got it, fine. Later that day Ken was acting like a jerk and trying to convince, her to go my ways and don't mix me up I am not but I just have a bad feeling about this ways, now your physic, I guess I am, nice to know, so can you predict the future, no but I would like too, but I cannot.

Later that day, Kelly and Ken were walking around in circle and now what? I am confused and I don't know which, I think it is lack of foods and water that is possible, yes it is. But don't worry I will find the ways and then it will be dark and then we will be stuck in the dark, think, I am, seem like you are not thanks for nothing, and then Ken somehow just slip and then Kelly grab him and but she was not too strong and but it was not too high and Ken was going to fall into the river, but somehow Kelly got him and he was safe and don't walk near the edge I told you time after time and you still think that you know what you are going and then Kelly notice that mudslide were getting to serious and we need to leave this area now and I think that we okay, but Ken said well I wants to use the path and where it will lead, I don't know. But then Kelly and Ken walk hand and hand and Ken hold tight and Kelly like that very much. Then he grabs her and kisses her tender lips and holds her tight, and don't let me. I won't let you go, and he remove her tee shirt and remove her bra and then put his lip next to her breast and lick them and suck them hard, and then he put her head between his legs and then she suck him and then they make passion love and then they were surrounded by zombies, and Kelly said this is a mistake that we make love. No, it is beautiful and I would like to do again. I don't think so, you not that hot, what? Kelly walk away from him and he pull her back, well you're a big tease, no I am not stopping saying, it is time fighting, the battle well I am not going gets caught in the woods and hide and quietly but I don't if I can I about to sneeze, hold your nose. About the zombies, they will be eaten up and our brain will be torn apart, stop this, I am trying, be alive, no sound and Kelly put her hand over his mouth.

Then he pulls her down and lay on of top of her and kept her mouth shut.

Kelly toss him off and make a scene and the zombies approaching, now they are getting closer, but then they passed by Kelly and Ken, but one zombie came back and Kelly, it was coming so close. But they duck down and been spotted and run, run I am. Kelly and Ken ran for there life and then the siren went off and it was hurting there head and covers ears.

But it was really like a warning sign and then they saw the house and we will go there, but Kelly and Ken didn't sees the cemetery, but they would approach the front but not inside, and Kelly said did sees anything, are you should? Nope your eyes playing trick on you, are sure? But then no sight of zombies, I am happy and it fine here, and we staying, I like that's well we will be warm and safe. We are staying, yes good idea, I like it.

Kelly walks in and sat and Ken walk in and then lock the door, this house is really old, but nice and old fashion, yes it is.

Later that night just resting and Ken fell asleep and Kelly head was on his shoulder, and both fast sleep, then Kelly woke up suddenly and saw a shadow and then shook him, and why did you wake me up? Because I heard a sound and seeing shadow. No, your eyes playing trick, no I am not doing that I really sees it, don't feel the chill, a little bit, it is from the draft, but we are fine. I don't sees anything your dreaming, no I am not I felt someone standing here; I don't sees anyone go back to bed.

At 3.00 am the clock went started to go off and shadow figures surrounded and something touch me, you touch yourself. No I didn't.

Yes did, and nothing.

NOWHERE TO RUN OR HIDE
BATTLE

DARK SHADOWS

Kelly got up and looks around the living room, and looking out of the window, and saw two shadow figures, and Kelly step out and walk the ground and saw the dark shadow and it came up and felt like it was going to bite her, but meanwhile Ken got up and looks around and he was not alone. Then something touches him and tries to pull him into the bottom of the floor, Ken was screaming for his life and Kelly was not hearing him, then heard sound try to walk inside but the door shut tight and then Kelly broke the window and when inside the house, and that moment Kelly saw the zombies coming from the cemetery toward her and she called out to Ken, but he was gone, so Kelly found some wood and fix the window to make sure that the zombies were not get in and then Kelly was inside the house and but seem like she was not alone and now Kelly was getting a bit scare and called out to ken, stop playing hide and seek and I don't want to be alone in the dark, and no answer from Ken, and then Kelly saw the shadow figures on the walls and they wanted to grab her and she somehow got away from them but now Kelly knew that she was not safe in the house and she cannot go out of the house because the zombies are waiting for her, and Kelly thought to herself and she had to find Ken, but those shadows were following her everywhere and at that point thought they were going to bite and she didn't know who she was dealing with. But now Kelly knew that she was in the haunted house and they don't want to let her go but they must have taken Ken, but there was a chance to get him back, but how where is he I don't have a clue and then Kelly, and then Kelly secure the upstairs and then went to the basement and she notice the globe and it was a ghost but was it friendly at this point didn't know and now Kelly was calling out Ken where are you? Then she looked and she find his watch on the floor, let him go and then she heard voices and said I think that I can sees you and ken was like near the window, no you cannot be dead? I am not but I am limbo, but I do not have no escape and he was very weak and said you need to leave now, I cannot go because I am surrounded by zombies if you stay you will be stuck here for forever, no I won't tell how to get you free, they are holding me tight and then Kelly heard a big bang and the zombies were inside and now I don't have no place to hide, but stop, don't let them gets you, but be silent like in the woods, and listens to me, but you between to world the living and the dead, and I need to pull you out and have you back, no you save yourself do you understand? Yes but I don't wants to be on this journey alone, and Kelly hid behind the wall and thought it was the zombies but it was the military and then blew some furniture and then they found me and I knew that I had to warns them that the zombies are not to far away from us. But then they felt the cold inside and then they saw the lady in the black dress and one of the soldier follows her into the others room and she disappear and so did the soldier, and now Kelly was getting terrify that she was not alone in the house and had to leave, but then she saw that the table was floating and Kelly said I cannot stay here Ken., so she was about to step out and she stop in front of the zombie, and now what? She quickly turns back and now Kelly didn't know, and was like a little child decided to stays with the ghosts. Kelly had no choice at this time and Kelly knew that she had to stay overnight and then leave in the morning, but now she was seeing more than she wanted but still was not being there because Ken were protection from the ghosts and keeps from the zombies, but Ken said I am not exactly a ghost and not a spirit, I know and I am able to sees you, so now your seeing the dead, I don't know if that is the skill that I have, but I know that I will be safe here with you and I will figure out how to save you and gets you back. Hope that you can, but I know that you try and I know that you are truly my friend. I know if I was not were having gone all ready, I know Kelly.

Then she saw his lifeless body in the library and Ken does not know that he had passed and Kelly was not about to tell him but Liza did and said you are one of us,, to Ken, and he said that is a lies, looks and you will be able to walks there the walls, no I cannot, yes you can. So he listens to Liza and when through and he said well, bye, bye my friend, Kelly. No, you cannot believe her, but now I do remember what happened to me. What you got murder in the house by ghosts,, yes and if you stay you will do that is nonsense and you don't believe me, listen do think that I wants to live in this house, that I thought that I was going home and we were chase by the zombies and now they very close and then you might not get home and you will be living in this haunted house, no never I will make it and I am a fighter, and I will not give on my life. The lighting stuck the house, and then it started to burn and said Ken said this is your chance to escape and promise that you will not comes back, I won't if I thought I were be able to save you were comes back because you're my true friend., so go now and don't cried for me, I won't but I do miss you very much,, so do I said Kelly, I will go and close the door behind me and but Kelly felt that someone touch and said it was you? No, I am next to Liza and I am going to her place, and she step out and looks around and then she was trap with zombies, and Kelly walks around them and try not be seen, but the little zombie girl spotted her and make a sound and they were chasing Kelly, and Kelly ran and ran for her life once again and fell into the grave and it was pitch dark and now thought she was going to be dead, someone threw the rope to her and she grab it and got pull up and then got to the top and then he said well I am glad to help you miss.

Let me introduce myself, Rick and I was coming through and I heard your scream and then I saw the zombies and so I fired the shot and now come with me and will be your bodyguard, well I don't need one,, well did you travel alone? No I was not alone but my friend died in that house.

HOUSE OF THE DEAD

Rick started to talked about the house and the history how many were murders and never found and the police of missing persons and composed bodies, and there were a lot Skelton in the basement, before the virus hit, and they said that was the house that ghosts to kept with someone go in and they never comes out, but I did, so you were lucky. You must had a friend that probably protection and that why your alive to talked about it. Well we need to leave this area, and now we will just drive away and you didn't bring alone out from there? I don't understand?

Then Kelly asked where are we going? Far away from here, okay but where not sure at this time but I just don't like being here, and then he stop and you brought someone out from the house and Kelly said no I have not, but It is not letting us leave, explains that's I cannot.

About one hour the car broke down and they were not too far from the house and it is wanted you and maybe I just should go by myself, you're not going to leave me alone? You need me, no I don't, get out of my car now, and soon has she did the car started up and said sorry, I need to go and you are going to leave me with the ghosts and the night of the living dead? Yes, but take my advice don't go back inside your going to abandon, me what kind of man are you? Then he said I think the ghost is clear get inside hurried and I will drive fast, I don't understand you must be a crazy man, no but you do sure sound like one, thanks a lot when I am getting you away from this hell, about hour half and they got into the highway, and out of the woods. Which direction, and well I came from south and now I will go toward north and then going to Virginia and then we can lay down on the beach and what then? Well we will think have something, well okay, and I thought it will be safe. Kelly agrees and so I like the idea and about further, away and Kelly was a little relief, but just thought about Ken. But then Kelly said why don't we get the highway and it will be quicker. But then she put on the radio and then heard "special news and said the zombies were going out of control and don't go into the big city and stay away for your own safety. What do they mean do not go there, to stay away, fine. Kelly said well I left my gun at the house and now I don't have a weapon. And how will I fight, well missy I will help you, what happen if you get infection, and don't called me missy, and name is Kelly,, the survive from the first virus that hit, okay I don't wants to hears it. but your not going to stop me how it happen first time well I was in the field and then my groups got slaughter in the field and eaten up and torn into pieces, and blood splatter, and I don't wants to hears the worst disaster, well I know, fire and burning building, and the quarantine I know and I was trapped, yes I heard many stories.

But I was one that was fighting and then I fell a few times and I got up and then I got some rescue from the Special Forces.

Follows By The Undead

What are you saying? Yes the ghost follow us and I didn't wanted to scare you but one did, well I don't like it. No they are in the backseat in the car, you must kidding, looks, you are right how did they get inside. Well back at the house we enter the car, and you didn't see us, no we didn't.

Looks what following us, not just ghosts and zombies too and they are too far from us, and I don't like it, I don't neither. But we just need to continue on this road and get out of here. I totally agree with you, Kelly and I feel the creep here and it not ending here, hope not.

Then the car stall and Kelly said now what so the rest of the ways we need to walks and I don't like walking because the zombies will catch up with us about the ghosts that are in our car so do we with them. Well I don't know I only deal with zombies and not the ghosts, well now you have too.

Don't push, I am not, well you are and we are stuck in the middle of nowhere, that is true, so we just keeps walking and walking and walking and we are out foods and clean clothes and then my shoes are worn out and I just don't like it here, I get it and stop repeating yourself., fine.

Kelly just stop and Rick said well don't gets it, we will died here, and you cannot stop and taking chances of ours life, but I am exhaust and tired, I am the same and we are being chase by zombies and ghosts and I don't know why you when into the house, well Ken and I were stranded and thought it was a good idea but became disaster and you came along and you save me, yes and then you lose your friend Ken, and I loss a few friends, on the ways and then we can just travel and not be seen, no we will be seen by the zombies and we are attach to the ghosts and it mean that they wants us to go back to the house and that were be fatal.

131

So, neither way we end up being dead, don't think that ways but yes! Stops it now, yes I will and I am too tired to walk and I just wants to sit here and get eaten up by the zombies, now you are acting a little crazy, but you are exhaust and we will find a place to stay, and without ghosts and zombies, so where is that place? I don't know yet! But when I see it and I will tell you, and but the ghosts were still with them, when they cross the border they were gone, and Rick said now we don't have to worry about the ghosts right now they didn't come with us, and Kelly said that is a relief, yes it is. But still have to worry about the zombies, they are not too far apart from us, and that is easy, what? We just have to shoot them in the head, and they were be dead, well where are the gun and bullets?

Oh! I see you don't have a gun and we don't have anything to protection our self and that is not good. Later that night, Kelly just looks around and then I see "boathouse" good and maybe we can stay there! Not sure at this point but I sees inside and you stay watched outside, why am I taking the dangerous task and you get the inside job?

I think I need to check it out and sees if we can stay the night here!

END OF THE ROAD

Rick went inside and Kelly stood and was shaking and nerve and then looks around the boathouse and then when inside and then Rick said I told you to stay outside, but why it is clear and I want to be here.

Fine, I guess I will have to check it out and Kelly said you don't have too I all ready did, fine then he sat on the boat and said do you know how to sail? Of course I do and we can just leave this area and go some place else, yes and I thought going back to Seattle, okay, I don't wants to stick around here, I don't neither, but Kelly then thought is that a good idea, yes leaving this location and we can just sail on the lakes and go north, okay I am in, I thought were in all ready? Okay.

Then Rick took control the boat and they both jump inside and Rick started up and they were on there ways. Then Kelly is taking the right direction to right to Seattle? Yes and I think that they have lab and clinic to help the epidemic, yes and maybe we can go back to LA? I believe that is a bit risk, well so is Seattle, well are we going? Yes of course and don't stall the boat on the lakes and no one will rescue us.

Are you sure? Yes I think that we are the only survivors and I think we will be the only that build the world back, well, maybe.

But Rick was a bit confuse with the compass in the boat and he was aiming the wrong direction and Kelly caught him and said let me drive the boat and we will land in Seattle and meanwhile the zombies were on near the boathouse and I am happy that we are not back there.

Now the breeze of the water was coming in and the Kelly said cover up. Okay I will take the blanket and I will be warm, good.

But Kelly notice that the boat was getting water inside the boat will we make too Seattle? Yes we will and don't worry about that's!

Then the temperature was changing and I don't like this at alls. Something is going on and I don't know the reason and but I think that we might be danger; I don't understand there must be global warning, and what else? Don't ask and I don't tell, I need to tell and I just want to know what you are thinking. Sound like we will run into some kind of disaster ahead, shut up, but don't says shut up but it is true, I went through something like that in the past and I think something bad going to happen here. Huh! Damn you don't even listen to me and the boat ride was great but the compass is broken and I don't know where we are going. Well it might be better than here, I don't know with the wind and then rain that is falling. but it looks like ashes, like from a volcano, what in these part? The world is changes and earth is moving and so I cannot explains it now.

Just be quiet and we will be fine, if you say so. I do and silent and not a word, okay! Silent when they sail the boat up stream, Kelly was seeing water was steaming and the boat was like breaking apart and Kelly said well we need to go shore now, but why we will burn up in this water.

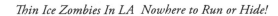

NOWHERE TO RUN OR HIDE!
BATTLE

VOLCANO ERUPT

Kelly said to Rick step out of the boat and don't fall into the lakes, and you will burn up and I don't understand what going on? I don't know but the lava flowing and it is in the water and don't sees the zombies faces burn into crisp? Yes I do, and we can end up that way. Well now we need to get to city away from the volcano and I don't know where it is safe or not. But the water is bubbling and if we step into the water we will burn up and I know that I am not stupid but we need to get far, far away from here now, got it and I just wants to be in the middle of the lava and the zombies and then we will have no place to hide, you means that we will be caught in hot lava and the zombies and no escape that is correct. So doesn't stand there and just keep on walking and we will be fine and then safe, we will be never safe, if the lava and the virus is spreading, that is true. Watch your step and don't go forward and then I don't what I am saying but I just want to say that we are in some time of trouble and I don't know how I will works it out, come on, Rick, we will climb higher ground and then we will go the other direction, yes and then around the trees and then far from the mountain, yes then what? Well we will be far from the boiling water and lava and don't step near the there what do you mean? Don't see it, it is like a half zombies dragging out the water, no, I didn't sees it but he turns her head and now do sees it? yes and gross, no kidding, but it is and go and don't looks back but the ground is not solid but really hot, hot, yes the lava flowing and it making the earth breaking into pieces, yes and I sees a hole in front of me,, yes and it is growing, yes I know, stop talking and I need to find a safer place, well there is no place like that's! I hear sirens and sees helicopters flying above us, and then it was silent like dead. But we still have to walks miles and miles and I hears

138

more helicopters and they are not looking for us but we are on own and you understand what I am saying? Yes but we cannot be the static but we need to survive this, we will and don't worry your little head, I don't have a little head, don't you that I was just kidding, no this is really serious stuff is happening and I don't want to died, you won't we will be rescue, how do you know and everything in sight it is melting and breaking, and I am really sick and I think that I cannot walks any further, don't give up Kelly, I am losing it., no you are not.

Comes on we have about ten miles and then we will end up in the city with Peoples, but hope not with zombies, no it will not be the case and I think soon we will be out of Seattle and we are going to Las Vega, is that good, it must be better than here, I agree, me too.

Then Kelly had to hold on too Rick and said hold me and I think that I am not able to walks any further, what wrong, I think I somehow hurt my ankle, not now, I will carry you, no thanks! I am a big girl, but you are walking too slow, well maybe I am but that is my speed. No it is not who are you fooling? You, well you are not. Then she just sat down and yawns and said I am going to sleep, no you cannot why not? Looks they are around us. Tree are crackling and falling into firewood and then they are coming toward us and I will be rolling down the mountain and Kelly said we are not alone and I see peoples down the mountain are you sure? Yes, maybe they are zombies, no they are just like us, fine, hope that you are right and seems like they are coming this ways and I think they might be zombies, no they do speak and they do walks like us, you really could tell, I cannot,, yours eye sight is great, but your survive are not, just keeps walking away and we will not gets hit by the tree, okay, but my feet are aching and I do need to rest but not now, don't sees the ground it hot and what coming out of the ground, yes they are zombies in multiply, yes and we are moving very slow and they can eat us, you mean our brain, because they are in pain, yes because the virus is spreading and they are growing, yes we when through that all ready, stop it.

Rick stops and looks around and then Kelly said well you cannot stop here and they will comes up and then they will gets us.

But listen and follow my steps and then turn the corner and try to reach the branch without falling, sure I think that I can do that's of course you can and I will just hold on too, won't the branch break? It strong and hard and it will hold both of us, well yours not lying about that's I were gets killed too, you know but we will be fine.

Take the rope and then put your hands together and then pull yourself over the rope and cross the river and then, and we will be on the safe side, yes, and we will not be in danger about those peoples,, we cannot help them, they are on there own, don't you get it, well maybe they do need our help and so your going to there and lose your chance to be sate and warm, you wants to help them. Yes, well I am going said Rick.

Be my guest, you can go myself and I am going to level land and were it doesn't crack and broken ground,, but you still need me to help you too go across, not really I figure a plan, well go Kelly, we are on our own now. Bye Rick, Kelly when across and said, folks I will help you out but then she notice that they were not alive and then she somehow got to Rick, and he said what wrong? You were right! I told you so, they were zombies, yes and I am going with you and you make the wrong decision and you were have ended up dead, yes, yes, yes, okay I will help you yes you're my friend and don't you ever leave me again, I won't and I wants to get out here before it get dark and creepy, me too, let go hurried and they were hiking out the wood and then they stop and they saw the cross road and which ways are we going, well straight out of the woods and flowing lava and it still burning my feet, mine too.

For three hours they were hiking out of the woods into civilization, and Kelly, well now take a break, yes we can because the coast is clear, are sure, yes, sorry repeating myself.

CEMETERY OF THE DEAD, COMING BACK TO LIVE

That day they walks about ten miles, and they were like the end of the road and nowhere to go so they decided to go into the cemetery and but Kelly said going into the cemetery when the dead comes out of the graves, is not such a good thing, well I think that we will get cross town and then we will be able to go inside and they are probably not there, so they are gone, I think, because they roam the streets of Las Vega, no-way yes ways and you don't believe, the graves are empty and okay start walking and walking and don't looks down. Oh they might jump out. Well; now we are heading toward the exit of the cemetery and then we climb the tree over the fence and then we will be inside of Las Vega, well you know your ways, sure I do and you don't missy, I hate when you called me that, Rick. About ten minutes later, Kelly said stop touching me, I am not but who is? It was an ugly zombie that was about to put his teeth inside and bite me and I just pull away and threw him into the ground and threw dirt on top to buried that zombies and the corner of my eye, I saw a little zombies girl coming toward me and I didn't wants to make a sound and then I hit the girl with the stick and then she fell to the ground and she was dead, and Rick said, at that moment I thought you were been dead but you somehow to manage to get out alive. Yes I did.

About one hour later, they saw the walker coming closer and closer, and what are we going to do? Well run into the woods, we just came out of them and I do wants to sees the city lights, of Las Vega, so do I just go.

They enter into Las Vega and they saw the lights were bright and Kelly couldn't believe that once that she won a lot of money there and probably now the slot were gone, and the zombies are the own the casino places, and Kelly was a bit disappointment, yes but I am willing to step inside and sees if I am lucky to win, but who were pays me out if I won. But Rick said first looks around and then go inside and you don't know who hiding, and then ten zombies jump out and then Kelly started to blast them and then Rick did the same and then said let go before we get chew, we won't I am the best zombies killer, well don't be a smart ass, I won't but now you acting like you know everything but probably you do but I still wants to help out if I can, you are.

Later that night, Kelly said well the zombies are gone and now I can play my ███████████████████████████████████████ generatio██ try the slots, well I don't think, I am going to watched the doors, in case if they decided to comes inside, well no sign of them make me a drink, vodka and orange, well you mean screw driver, yes.

What are you going to have? Well nothing but maybe a bud light!

That all you going to have and then I will check the suite and then I am going to bed, but I thought you were going to be my guard, well I am exhaust, so am I, let have some fun, not now. Well I am too sleepy, and going to sleep are you going to join me, no way I am going to play double diamond, okay you are on your own, fine and went I finish playing I will comes up, then Kelly saw a shadow and thought it was Rick but it was zombie, and torn into pieces. Kelly bend down but seen her and Kelly got up and ran push button, up and it open up and step inside and the zombies, then it got the right floor, step out and ran inside the room.

Later that they bolt door and stay in bed and this was the worst idea coming here, I think your right. But the morning and leaves this place and found a car in the garage, yep about car well out gas and the engine blow. Can we fix that I don't think so, now what I told you search and then we will gets away and we will be safe from sin city.

Well it "Sin City" because of the gambling, well I do like gamble but with circumstance, I cannot, deal that the zombies are winning and we are losing, no we are not. But Kelly you're losing your mind, I am so stupid I left the money in the machine, I should go back and get it, you don't need the water and there was sirens and air raid and the street and were blow up, and burning and now we need to go. No, I am going back and watched my back, of course I will, go if your money hungry and you could end dead, go for it, I am I work too hard to leave it, you are sick.

Stop calling me that, no I am not going allowance to go your not my keeper and you are acting childish.

Kelly didn't and went unharmed and Rick follow her into the slot room, and went to the machine and took the money, and one zombie was one inch away from, but I will pull her away and I was going to gets bitten and then he slam the zombie down and ran for his life, and you know what you did? Yes I got the money in case that we need it and that why, money is worth nothing now. Then Rick saw some fancy blue BMW, and step inside and press to start up the car and drove away and Kelly said are you driving over 100 miles per mile are you trying to killed us, but sure seem like it. But I am not but I am trying to escape the zombies and we would be safe but your going back to LA , it is infection with zombies, yes, no maybe a good place to safe among zombies and we blend in. I don't think so, and then we will get shot in the head, bad, bad idea, I agree.

But we have no choice but we still going there, but will be okay I am not sure, I believe that there is no place to hide.

Now your telling the truth, I knew that's but I think that the location, will be secure and then we don't have plan, no I don't but don't be furious with me, but all the times we get into trouble time after time by going into places that we are not able to get away and then we get hunted by the zombies, and I am sick and tired of this ordeal, don't think that I am the same, yes at I did it much longer than you, well I think at this point about average, well I am the professional solider with killing skills, well I am the scientist with working on the antidote and fighting for my life too.

PRESIDENT AND HIS FAMILY

Meanwhile Kelly and Rick were racing for time and there was a special report that the President of the united states got attack by zombies and his family and they don't know if they survive the attack, at this time, well I see the president, might not be alive because the epidemic, and somehow the zombies got inside the white house and probably chew them up. But I hope not but if that the case. What else are they saying and not much and it is top secret, probably it is. Well I think that the danger is not over and I believe that it is continue with any help.

Secrets services, walking in but they became to be like zombies and then more peoples were killed, and then know one will be save and what are they saying about the vice president, well he is a goner, well he got eaten up by the zombies, because he was face to face and nowhere to run.

But about five hundred are dead in the white house and more body counts that is terrible and I don't believe it. But are the military are in forces and we are dooms stop saying that's and then what I just stop it. Do you hear what I am saying, we cannot stay here, and we cannot hide from the zombies, that are true, but I think that we just should just move on and then we will be good, well I guess so. But staying and being a target.

I will not be a target for anyone, especially me and you. Well get back into the car and we should go into country and then maybe be at some farm, well maybe it will not be so much zombies around and we will be easy killing them off, yes but we need to find out if the president is alive and his family, who will run the country if he and his family are dead?

That is a good question Kelly but there is no solution to this problem and it will be a martial law and maybe they will think that we are zombies and they will kill us too, shut you, you crazy bitch, I am not a bitch.

But you are no prince charming Rick, without me, you were not make it, don't flatter yourself, well it is true, said Kelly to Rick.

But Kelly walks back and said well I am not going to the east coast but I am staying here, once again your making the wrong decision and whatever I make it will not be right for you, just go and I will go back to my home and I will sit and wait until this epidemic is over, no you cannot do that's, why not? Because they will smell you and break inside and bite you, it doesn't matter and I am staying and you stubborn, maybe I am but that what I am going to do and I will listen to the report and if I need to move I will and you can go and don't feel bad and you are not responsible for me, do you understand? Yeah! Go get out my hair, no you are coming, don't force me, I will fight with you, but I am trying to save you, I will be fine take my word, I am but you still must comes with me. Okay I will, but there is no place to hide, I know but you were be trap here, I don't care and I were make it, no you are fooling yourself, no I am tuned into reality, in some sense I am but I am willing to stay home and deal with them myself, go Rick and he came up to her and kissed her and gave her a hug and it was peacefully and said I am going to leave you for a while, don't let me stop you, I won't. about one later Rick when out and Kelly lock up the door and sat and looks at that empty screen and waiting for any update what happen at the white house and heard moaning and groaning and Kelly looks out of the window and Rick was surrounded by the Zombies and Kelly at that point didn't know what to do, but just kept watching and looks like he was going to make it and then a little while the firecracker when off and he somehow ran way and didn't looks back at me and I knew that he got into the car and left me with my choice of not going, and I just sat and thought when they were going to gets me, but still stare out of the window of her home and Kelly started to think about her the good thought and the love that she once had and didn't wants to forget that some day it will be never the same but probably were be better and then she thought I were have the cure that this kind of crisis were not occurs again, she thought and daydream, about being marry to Joe but he loss the battle with the zombies and were not sees him again, but didn't give up that Kelly were make it and her life were be better with someone new and would not work for the government and they lies to her time after, and then had to go out to the field and got caught up in the middle of the battle and no one help

145

her and was almost killed and one thing she knew that she was not a static of being dead, but almost got infection but the antidote work and make it and seeing the sky was blue but the street of red of blood.

Kelly started to change her clothes and doing routine, and resting for a day and then meanwhile Rick struggle and fight off the zombies and but didn't really make it, but was wound but not bit by the zombie, but one soldier shot at him hurt his arm and it was bleeding and the zombies started to smell the blood and they were coming close to Rick.

But then the helicopter were coming and shooting at them and then they shot me, near my head and I suddenly fell down and one of the soldier jump out of the plane and they wanted to hunt me like I was a zombie, but I was not and then they spoke to me and I answer and now they pick me up and took me to the hospital to cure me. But those doctors were not friendly and they asked me questions and I was afraid to answers them at that time and I was silent. Then the lights when out and it was a moment that I need to run and the zombies broke in and I ran and ran and the soldiers got eaten up and I took the jeep and I drove away and I didn't looks back until I was out of there and the fire was burning and I thought I should go back to Kelly, and now Rick was trying to remember the way to her home but was confuse and daze with the medicine in his system, but he didn't give up and somehow he was in front of Kelly home and just had to remember what floor? My blank and I don't remember. But Rick knock at every door and called out her name and then I heard her calling out my name and I follows the sound and I was right next to her door and I knock and she said who is this? Rick, why did you comes well there are a whole bunch of zombies and I don't wants to dies, okay I will let you in but first I need to check out for bite marks, I don't have them, how do I know. Then she check him out and said well you don't have any marks but hurried to get inside and it is terrible news that the president and his family got slaughter in the "white house" they didn't have time to go into the shelter, because the zombies just attack and killed them and now the country is under marital law.

You are saying we are under martial law, they are allow to shoot and then asked questions, and they don't care if you are not a zombies or not. But zombies don't have mind but we do., well if you wants out there again your probably will get shot and in the head, more detail at the white house, they are showing what happen, well seems like they are alls dead, you are right, so how many did survive that attack and then the TV when into emergency alert and that is not good and we don't even have a president, they are all dead at the white house and who is running the country? Huh! The zombies of course, how do you know, well looks outside and what do you sees, well just zombies roaming the streets, do you sees any living soul out there? No, I don't. Well I guess we are the only one and maybe the military, at this point I don't know. Just being silent and don't make a sound and not to alert the zombies, so did they follows you, I don't but I really try to be quiet and snuck inside the building, not sure.

Well, hope that no one follow you, me neither, said Kelly.

Then Kelly and Rick sat on the couch and he started to touch her hand and then he wanted to kiss her, but he slaps his face.

Why did you do that's? Well seems like you were taking advantage of me, but I am not, well it just felt like it, sorry.

Then she stood up and looks out of the window and saw tank coming through and zombies falling down and then shooting, explosions all around and Kelly heard a crackling sound from the roof and then I think this mean we cannot stay here, we cannot leave, we must go, this building will fall on us, how do you know? Looks at the walls, yes I sees but they seem fine, but the interior and out surface, it not solid, well you know your building, yes once I when to school to be an engineer but then I decided to become scientist, well you are really smart, thanks, Rick.

Kelly peek through the hole and went I count to ten we are leaving, yes we immediately, I will be the first one that step out of my apartment and you follow me, Yes and we will not be taking the elevator down and we will takes the steps down, okay, because the elevator could have got stuck on the floor and no one would rescue us, yes.

But hurried the coast is clear at this moment, well I think it is, and about a minute later, they were coming toward us and I was about to scream.

BRINGING OUT THE DEAD

The moment that they were about to step out, Kelly and Rick saw that they were carried out bodies out of the building and some were still struggle and fighting and Rick wanted to go out and help them but Kelly said don't go out they will shoot you, I know but those peoples are still alive, no they are not they are zombies,. How they twit and move and don't speak, you cannot be sure, yes I am. Kelly and Rick waited for them to leave and Kelly said stay by the walls and don't be seen. Okay, and I will do the same, and we will not be killed, but one thing I need to go back inside of my apartment and I have left vital information on the disk and I need to get it and give to the government, your going to risk your life and they might killed you, yes I am. Fine I will wait for you near the stairs. But it took a while and Kelly couldn't find it but it fell down near the desk and said, here it is, and took and walks out and walks downstairs and then when right to Rick and said now we can go and we will be safe and I think some road are roadblock, you are right.

Yes, how do we gets inside., well maybe we can sneak inside and then we can just go inside and then we can among with them but not with the dead that is correct, yes I know but somehow confuse, well still we are going and I think that we will be fine, I am not stay behind, I am going to follow you and hope that we don't get shot, I don't neither, I agree.

But Kelly had a bad feeling about going there and she knew it was the wrong choice, yes but I think this is the city of the dead, how do you know that, don't you sees it? not exactly but I think there are no zombies, are you blind, don't sees them, chewing up body and the soldiers getting slaughter and into tiny pieces, and they are chanting we wants brains, and don't you sees the drool that coming out there mouth, and they are just like rabies dog to eat the brain, because there head hurt and they wants to eat the brain because it stop for awhile, well yes but we have weapons and we will make it, yes you sound like sure about yourself, I am and I am a surviving and don't realize what I am saying, yes, but is it true and do you have a motive about going there? yes to gets supplies and move on, but we were once barricade and I think that I want that again, we won't and do you guarantee that we won't gets killed? I don't know how to answer that but keep on moving and don't be scare, sure, I will go and take a chance, but I am not going too died, no you will not. But also you cannot predict what will happen and don't be a jerk, I am not.

Kelly said well, well I am going and you better save my ass, I will and don't be a drama queen, I am not but how you are doing thing that will put us in jeopardy and I don't like it at not alls.

Rick said you have trust me in the past and now you should trust me again, I am but don't let us died here, no, no, no, it will be okay! But you know your ways, but looked out, they are approaching us, bend down and they will sees you, listen to me and don't let them sees us they will attack us, I do know they can smell us, you right and one is coming toward us and now he is making a sound to alert the others zombies, what have done? Nothing, the zombies smell you and now he is calling his pack.

Now bend down go toward the truck and then try to get inside and sees if there are keys and we can we drive away and I jump inside and then we just then about a minute later., Kelly was about to be caught and then Rick took out the gun and shot about ten zombies and blew there head splatter all around the street, good job, Rick, you save me, I said I would, I know and you never let me down, and you protecting me, well it is time to kiss but just go, and then Kelly said sped away and then he did and the thousand zombies were very close. But then the truck stall and then they saw soldiers marching toward them, what do you think? Are they alive? No they are zombies, how you know, watched how they are walking. Yep you know your zombies, Rick, why are we not we moving, well the we are out of gas. Looks at I am why are we having so much trouble, I don't know but we need to run, you better, move your ass, I am but you one son of bitch that got be into so many troubles that I never had before, and I was a battle and I do have scar but still I am not fighting.

So am I Kelly and we will get home but we have no home to go back too. That is true but we will soon, this epidemic will not last forever.

But Kelly hold his hand and let started walking out fast out of dodge, but will we make it? Are you having doubt? At this moment and I think I am having a melt. But you need to be strong and not to be afraid.

I am not, and Rick hold her tight and then Kelly said let go now, I am but I just want to leave, fine Rick said, don't walks fast but don't alert the zombies, don't tell me the drill, and I know how you have to be quiet and not loud, well I am not, but seems like they still sees us, well we need to run now, yes, I totally agree, me too.

But suddenly Kelly stops and Rick said what are you doing? I wants to sees if they will pays attention to me, you don't want be caught? No but I just want to sees what happen, are you suicide? No I am not but maybe some distract, well but you showing them that we are here and they are coming, are you nut? Nope, but I just wants to use the antidote on that zombie, no, don't do it, I need to test it, your on your own.

But one minute later, and the zombies were about one hundred feet from the zombies, one zombie was crawling on his body and a bloody mouth.

Then the arms came out and then pull me down and bang and he was dead and now they were coming toward us and Kelly said go inside the dress shop? What?

CITY OF DEAD

Couples shots came and Kelly and Rick were inside and said who was shooting at us, no I cannot believe these zombies, having weapons, no now we are deep shit, yes and you were the one wanted to go inside, I know.

Firecracker flying up and bright lights, and the zombies was looking up and it was a distract, and we could escape from here and we will be safe. But then go, right now because they are busy, now it is time, let move now, go around the bend and the fence, and climb it over and jump over, jump now, I am they are not looking and I want to go but I am frighten, and but you shaking body but I will protection you, you will?

The city of dead, are a whole a lot of zombies, but you know they are starving and they wants to eat our brains, yes keeps on moving, I am and I will not be fine, and we will be middle of the zombies.

But they were surrounded and I thought we were not but we are.

Don't you sees them they are stare at us, and they are coming closer to us and we need to go inside, now, I don't see a opening, do you?

Now, run, run, I am back of you, are you Rick, I am fine, are sure, because your leg is bleeding, yes must been bitten and you will be infection, no I am not, I just got cut on the wire fence, I don't think so.

I will check it out and if your not bitten, you will not be quarantine, I will be with you, I know you, you are so special to me and I do like you and I don't want to lose you, you won't, but you don't know that's? But I believe that I will be fine. But I am not sure that you will be. Let me check your leg and I can but some alcoholic and then rub it and get the bad germ out, well I will save your leg and spreading the infection.

I need to give you a blood test and then look if the cells are multiply,

151

but now you scare me, don't be, maybe I can try the antidote, and well I don't want the shot, what you told me about it, that might get me sick.

"The smoke is coming in and I don't see anything in front of me and I don't like it but we have no choice and we need move and then we can be safe, and yes but the smoke is dark and I don't want to be here, do I! no I just want to leave this area but too smoky and I cannot breathe and you know that is so bad, don't collapse on the ground they will grab you drag you too the crowd, I know but still is too bad here and I am not sure if we will make it this, stop being so negative, I am trying my best but I am thinking the worst and then there was bang and then a explosion and fires around and they were in the middle of the war between the soldiers and the zombies and no escape, yes we will get out the "city of the dead" I just know, well I am not and I am getting weaker by the moment, you are giving up, no I am not! But sure it seems that ways, stop, whining like a child, I am not acting like a child and I just wants to get the hell out of here. So do I and I don't wants to perish here, I really don't wants too.

Well, somehow you convince that this place were be safe but turn out to be our place to dies, we are not dooms, so far we are not and I don't want too be, do you understand? Yes but we are going into circle and there is no opening space to clear out, there must be, well so far I don't sees it, well you will, and today we will not dies here, how do you know that we will not? I don't but stop it, now!!!!

"Promise me, you will not abandon me and run when you have the opportunity, well I won't I will be on yours side and I will get you safe.

Well, I do believe you, to a point, and I think that you are honest and I will be fine, and I will not be nervous, that good to hears.

When they started to walks and walks away and seem like it was getting better and then the smoke was disappearing and now Kelly was relief and now we have to deal with an obstacle ahead of us, what is it? Well there is a tank and a lot of zombies ahead and I don't know we will be able to get to the tank and then what? Then we will be able to shoot them and we will be able to travel out of here with the tank that is some heavy equipment to drive, I know but this will get us out this town and then what? We will be spotted and then the military and shoot out of water, that is nonsense. well no it is not and I think it will help us and the zombies will not catch us. They still can but I am not going them inside the tank and then I will just keeps on driving to the coast and we will be away from cease fires and then we will be able to get another transportation and then we will go to Chicago and we will gets some help, do sees the thin ice zombies, they are furious and hungry and they wants "brains" I hears that quickly started this tank up and I wants to get the hell out of here now. But it won't start and I think they will be trap in the middle and I don't like be a meal for the undead, do you think that I do? No I don't. Don't be a bitch. I am not and I did better when I was alone, well leave I am not stopping you, go but I cannot go because I will be caught, well I know I was testing you. I should just pinch with the antidote and then sees how you act with shot; you are not going to give me that antidote and you how the side effective is? Yes and I don't want that bad reaction, I don't blame you. But you don't realize you might get the virus and I am taking my chances. Yes I know and I think it will be fine, but not sure, you are confused. No I am not confused I am fine.

Listen to the sound it is an air raid and I think that they are planning to blow this section of town, and no the whole city.

Later it started like a lot missiles were firing in the sky, and I think that they will blow this tank and one zombie somehow jump on the tank and then try to go inside and I took a steel bar and then I hit the zombie off and I close the door and the air was awful and saw bodies on the tank and I told Rick and we need to remove them they might wake up and venous us,, hurried, but check it out if it is clear, I think it is and then the bomb blew a whole into the tank and we cannot be here, I know.

End Of The Line

Now what? Be patience we will escape from here. how do you know, I just know. What do you think this is the end, but I think that we will be fine?

Seem like we are just going around in circle but we are still in the same place that we started, yes and what do you wants to says about that's are going to get defeat by the zombies, one thing I will try not too, and I will defense you and we both will make out from here, but we have no place to go, just like a minute later the rain came down and the wind blowing and then the lighting hit the building and then it started to sparkle and then the sun came and then rainbow and then we looks and but we were surprise but then they came the zombies and I was froze on the street and Rick try to pull me, but I couldn't move.

Now, something happen and I just started to move very quickly and I couldn't focus on anything, I knew that I could keep on fighting, the strength and energy was gone and I couldn't go on and at that moment, I wanted to tell Rick, to let me go and I would be alone.

But then the mist came and then it got really foggy just like a second, and I didn't mention today is the day it end. What? I don't believe what you are saying; this is the end of the line. Not exactly but we will gets out of here, and then we can go toward the east coast and the epidemic, and we can live a normal live. Well one thing no more zombies and it will be fun to go to the theatre and dinner and then we can go dancing.

Well, it sounds like a dream that everyone is alive and then we can, go fun and not to worry about it. Well when we will will get there! Soon. I am asking how many days to the New York City? A few day, but we can take a plane, what? Are you serious? Yes I am and it will be quicker, are sure that the planes are flying? Well we should go to the airport and then we can check it out and that sound good, do you think that we will be seeing zombies, huh! Well not sure but I am willing to try me too, said Rick.

So keeps on talking and I will listen to you and I know that we will see other persons that are lives they will be happy to see us? You got it and but he was not telling her the truth about the destruction and devastation going on but the fear would scare her out of her wit and but he kept silent but she was not silent but worry about what was going around and seeing them coming toward. Rick hold her hands and then they were walking on the street and then they heard horns when from the cars, and now Kelly said I am dreaming, I don't know but car driving in the street and then about two hours, the sound was silent and then said what happen to the sound, and Rick said what sounds? I don't understand what you're saying? I heard car driving by, no you must been dreaming, no it was real.

It was really not lies to me, I am telling you the truth, no you are brainwashing, what no I am not I am trying to survive this battle like you.

Well, you are confusing me and you must be drugged me, what? Your delusion, no I am not and stop lying to me. Where are they? Who?

The persons were talking and the car horns that we blasting off, no ways you had a dream, like once it was, no that is not true where did they gone? You're scaring me, you need help, but the medical faculties are close and run by zombies. Take me there now, and I will show you that you were dreaming and you were not there, but once it was there.

No, I hate you for telling me fib and I know that I was there last night and you slip a Mickey in my drink, you had one water and you open the bottle by yourself, liar, no I am not stop fighting with me, take me home now, you cannot go now, why? I need to be there and wait for my family to comes home, do you have a case of anemia, well no but I just remember yesterday, well it was a beautiful day. Looks at the sun and the sky is blue.

About a minute later, she slapped his face and then said well how could you hit me, well like this, and once again, she hit him and he fell to the ground, and then got up and said you are one crazy chick.

I feel that I have a severe headache and you are not looking at great but are you all right? Yes I am but I think you need to rest, I am ready you need to take your time and I don't think so, I know I can go, no we are staying until you feel better, I am trust me, let go and I don't wants to be blame if the zombies attack us,, I won't. Comes on Rick I don't like that stalling I just wants to leave this area, do sees any roads that we can takes? No but I am willing to turn around and go east, but we might end up the same ways, comes and I don't wants to hears that from your mouth, and fine. But then suddenly Kelly started to walks and then wait a minute, I need you too hold me, I feel that I have some vertigo, what I don't understand, because the stress and what going on that bought it on, well I can help you but I don't know how, but they are coming closer and closer., and I am terrify and I think that we should run and I am not able to walks, just leave me, I will not, you will make it, sure.

One hour later, the zombies were not too far and they were just like a mile away and that is not good, I know. Listens if we do separate, I will find you and we will be together, are you sure that going happened? Yes I do. I will and you can takes my word and I am not a liar, I know you are not but how, are you? A bit shaking and cannot walks but try, I will, I don't wants to be dead meat, you won't be, take what I says. I will Rick.

Somehow Kelly got the energy and said I am ready to move and what happened, well I thought if I stay I would end of dead so I just thought of good things and then I got better, good so let go and don t let back I won't, and they walks and Kelly spotted a CRV and it was a silver car and Kelly said the key are inside and let drive away.

Then Kelly said this car has navigation, and we are on our way that is so awesome, yes and we will be save and not be torn into pieces, no we will not, and Kelly smiles and I know that we will find someone else who alive.

FULL MOON

Kelly and Rick drove for hours and hours and then Kelly wanted to stay at the bed and breakfast place and Rick said are you sure?

Yes, I never been a place that before, well looks at the sky the moon is full and I believe that things happen, like what? Don't say that zombies will roamed, no I was going says that we might run into werewolf. You must be kidding, and what they will turn us into werewolf? Yep around these parts of states and I don't know if they are real. That is true and I don't wants to become a werewolf, bad enough running into zombies that is really worry, so how are your symptom, none right now, that good, so they enter the inn and it was empty and no one was inside and Kelly looked around and grab a key and then said we will take room 7. Great lucky number, yes.

So check it out at the dinning room, and so we can put on some music and dance, but I don't wants to be notice from the outside world, there is no one out there, but we still have the zombies, that are true, yes it is.

But the night was getting darker and darker, are going have a "moon eclipse"? I don't think so, but let go to the bedroom and I hope that they have two beds. Me too and I don't wants to sleep with you my friend, well I don't neither, tell me the truth, you do want to sleep with me? Yes from day one, yes, yes, I will not deny my desire, fine.

Then Kelly heard something, what is it? I don't know. But I think we need to be quiet, I think you are right, but then Kelly said lock the door, I am and just sit quiet, and Rick was about to sees out in the hall, but it was a tiny dog and that started to bark and Kelly grab the dog and put on the bed and pat it and then Rick said it is a cute puppy? Yes it is, and then Kelly looked closer into the puppy eyes and then the dog became rabbit.

Then Kelly stabs the dog and threw it out and burns it and then Rick said what have you done? That dog is zombie, no are you serious? Yes I am.

This dog could have belong to a child and you killed it, well did you wanted to get bitten, no so shut up, well that child will cry, that child could be a zombie by now that is true. But meanwhile, we need to focus, and how to gets way in case that we are attack by zombies. yes but I think I saw something in the woods and I don't think it was a zombies I think we have werewolves out there, your mind is playing trick on you, no I am seeing that, sure you are but those are just shadow of the moon, I don't think so, Rick, and Kelly said well got your bullets ready and then if it a werewolves, and you need silver bullets, how do you know but I do. You can killed a werewolves with a silver bullets, and then with the zombies you shoot into the head, and with vampires, stake into the heart, well you know that we will not runs into vampires and werewolves? Tell me how do you know that we won't? I did. okay!

But then Kelly said I just seen something strange in the woods, I think that you are just seeing things and we don't have to worry about it, hope that your right? I am and then there was a banged at the door, they know that we are here, but who? Guess, I have no clue, okay don't panic.

Did you sees the bushes moving and I think we have a werewolves in the woods and I think you are wrong, but I don't think so but locked the doors and we will be fine, you think so and I will go to the basement, but you don't lives here and you have no right to there, well maybe they could be hint about the howling sound in the woods and how to killed the werewolves, but you means the zombies, no I mean the werewolves, well I don't think but you think we will be safe? Can we deal with werewolves and need to find silver bullets, you must be kidding and we cannot go out we will gets bitten and turn into a werewolves in this century? I don't think that is wise tale, but what is lurking out there? Well zombies.

I don't think so, so Kelly and Rick decided to go to the basement and then Kelly called out and said I think I find some silver in the basement and I think we will be protection and then we can leave this place in the house because the full moon will be gone, but why can just stay here, in some bed and breakfast place somehow in the woods that no street but dark woods and no peoples around, I don't think so.

About one hour, and Kelly said to Rick and said I will take the rifle and bring the bullets and then we can just go and we will have the weapons to fight off the zombies, and then we can have some kind of normal life.

But still we need to find out what is lurking out there and then we can fight it, yes but if it stronger than us and we lose, now you have doubt, no I don't but I am not moving and I am staying until morning, I don't wants to turn into werewolves, and then you will walks the night when the full moon comes out, yes and then you killed the innocence, well I don't wants to become a werewolves, do you think that I wants, so we need to filled up our tank and leave the inn and then we go someplace else?

But we are better off here and we should stay, no I am going now, Rick don't stay with me and I don't wants to be alone, I don't wants you get bitten and become a werewolf, I won't! How do you know anything, I don't but I just don't like it here, I feel that we are being watched. Are you saying being watched, I am sure, but please don't leaves and then Kelly said I am seeing things and like what? First place I thought it was werewolves but it could been zombies, not sure but just relaxed. I am trying, but be patience. Well I don't know what I am saying but don't open the door because it might comes in and what are you saying? You are confuse, no I am not but I am seeing a furry man in the bushes and big teeth, no, yes I am, don't you sees it? Briefly but not sure what?

Now what? What are we going to do? Well going stay put and not going out. I will stay with you tonight and the morning I am leaving you, that is fine, but the morning, I am going said Rick. Fine, but believe that I will be okay! But Kelly cuddles next to Rick and kiss his lips, and Rick gave a hug, and then hold her tight, don't let me go.

MORNING SUNLIGHT

Morning came and Rick got up and got dressed, opens the door wide and steps out on the porch and then sat on the porch, on the rocker.

Kelly came out and said what your doing your going to let the zombies in but you are saying that they were werewolves and now your speaking, about zombies, what was it werewolves, yes but now the morning and are you staying? No, after breakfast, I will be leaving, and Rick walks out into the woods, and saw footprints in the dirt and they are big, he called her over, what are those footprints, well werewolves would hunting for victims.

So if we steps out last night, then we would be there feast, well someway we are lucky, they could have attack and bitten us, but I had the door closed, so they were in a pack of wolves, that is really dangerous.

Rick said you can stay but I am going, you will have defended yourself. Fine, go, I don't want you here, and he left and didn't look back. Kelly step inside shut the door and sat down at kitchen table and then went to the gets some foods and smell the foods, then took a bite but it was spoil, and threw it out into the trash, and then Kelly got sick in the stomach,, and about twenty minutes, it was Rick, but was unable to open the door, but meanwhile Kelly, was lying on the floor, and then Rick broke the window and got inside and ran up to Kelly, and carry to the bed and put on bed on the pillow and Rick put a wet cloth on top of here forehead.

But Kelly still was out, but then Rick realized the door was wide open and it was getting dark and now I need to shut doors and not let the zombies inside, and went he was running and almost fell and Kelly was screaming like she was losing her mind. Rick is trying to lock the door and the broken window with some woods, then took a hammer and hammering hard but looking for nails and then Kelly got up and then came down the stairs, and Rick said what are you doing? I am trying to keeps the zombies out, and what else is lurking out there, because it was daylight, and they didn't need to protection from wolf.

Kelly said I will shoot those zombies back too hell. But they are too powerful to kill and not enough bullets well are we going to survive?

Yes we are going to make it, yes let me put the knife between there eyes.

You need to stab them into head, and they will dies.

I know they don't have brains, because there head hurt and them hungry for brains and relief the pain.

Do you hears the sounds that they are really hungry and we are stranded and no one will find us, that is true, but will we make it. Yes we will.

About two hours later, more zombies were coming inside, so let go upstairs and hide, and we will lock the doors behind us.

But Kelly was getting weaker and weaker and just passed out and Rick splash water, and put the chair behind on the door, and it was secure.

Then the banged and then Kelly woke up and said what happened? You don't remember? What? You didn't get bitten, no I don't think so, am fine, but I ate something that was bad,, yes and maybe it was infection foods, yes you could become a zombie, no ways, I just will take some pills from the lab that I had and I will be fine, are you sure? Yes, yes. I will be. Good to hear and I hope that you recovery soon, don't worry and I am glad that you back so am I. next time you listen to me, I will.

Yes I will but we don't have time to argue but time too runs and you are because any second they will attack us and so where did they came from, and I don't know but we are not safe here, no kidding, gets out the window, I barely walks and how can I climb down the window and I don't know but try, I am but you slow, but you something weird and I don't like it. But what do you means went I ate it and I just felt ill, no but what did you eat? I just had some pie and then some strawberry and cream and I got nausea and I cannot explain, well you and you looks better than before, well we need to escape this inn now, and we need to get to the car and speed away, do you understand what I am saying when you get down, you just runs to the car and then you started the car and I will be there. about a minute later he got into the car drove away, and the zombies following them, now the looks back and seems they were catching up to them oh my god. Now what? Keeps going and don't stops I am not, they were getting closer and closer but then somehow they end up in the ditch. Then they hit the tree and Kelly hurt her head and Rick got his leg stuck and cannot take it out, I will help but they are coming, Kelly needs your help, I will. I cannot get you out, what should I do? Well try to pull me out, I am trying your leg in stuck and I cannot pull it out but I sees the zombies coming and I will hide in the bushes and then I will sees where they when and then I will save you. But please hide I sees them, I will don't make a sound I won't but they are coming toward me, I need to hide under the steering wheel, and but they still sees me, no but Kelly somehow pull out the gun out of the trunk and started to shoot and then she saw wrench and pull it out and when to Rick and pull him out and then leg was in bad shape and then Rick said take me on the other side that they will not see us, I am trying but you are too heavy, sorry about saying that's well that okay, I guess, yes I know, but be quiet they still can smell us. I know but that why we need to take some off the dead zombie, and spread on ourselves, yes and they will not approach us, true.

But Kelly didn't know how she will get Rick out the woods with alls those zombies around and now the plan was to leaves Rick and Kelly search for help and rescue, but Kelly didn't know which direction to go but Kelly when back to Rick, I am sorry and I don't know how long I will be. But I need to go the hospital for medial supplies to help you and with the pain.

But also get you some clutches, and you will be able to walks, yes, I will sit in the bushes, and I will not make a move. Good!

ZOMBIES ARE COMING!!!

Meanwhile Kelly was on her way and thought that Rick were be fine and Kelly kept walking and walking and stop for a moment and then stop and looks back so far she could have seen Rick, and didn't wanted to yelled out and then kept walking and was very quiet. Meanwhile Rick was laying down in the bushes and was waiting for Kelly to comes back but now he knew that he had to drag himself because they were sees him and then he were be dead meat, and Rick refuse to be zombies meal so he somehow very quiet move and not making a sound, but a minute later Rick started to sneeze and they heard that, and now he was getting really scare that they might grab him, and Kelly was getting closer to the hospital and then had to find the right equipment but couldn't carry everything to him., and now Kelly had to make decision and hope they were the right one, and Kelly was thinking about Rick and worry that he probably got caught but hope not, and so she grab some morphine and some clutches and then got a wheel chair and was about to take it out and now Kelly realize that she saw zombies coming this ways.

Kelly, spotted a ambulance and put the stuff into the ambulance, and went inside and started up, but at first it won't , and then did and I drove off and was looking for location that she left, so Kelly went about five away and passed and not sure where Rick was, and saw in the back of ambulance, but then saw something in the bushes, and thought it was Rick and Kelly stops and got out and called his name but didn't answers and then saw them coming, jump back and started up and drove away. And meanwhile, Kelly looks around when she was driving, and saw Rick, and stops it and got out find him. She got the crutches and morphine, and gave the shot to him and he got tired and walking, walking, to the ambulance

163

and she put him inside the stretcher and lays there and Kelly drove off, but the zombies would coming closer and closer, and one zombie was about climbing the ambulance, and Kelly shook the zombie off. But then Kelly saw Rick trying to gets up, and Kelly said stay quiet.

But they are coming, I do sees them but I want to shoot them, but you are not well, just stay put, no I want to help you, well you are distract me, but be quiet, okay I will and the more miles they going more zombies to be mores, I cannot believe it, seems like we are surrounded and we are trapped, can you turn around? I should just runs them down and go through them, but Kelly can I do it? Yes you can, comes on don't give up I don't have the strength, well I don't want to dies here, you won't. How do you know, I don't know but I just want be out of this hell, so do I.

Meanwhile Rick still laying on the stretcher, and lift his head, no, no, no, one is inside, and Kelly stops suddenly. Then the zombie flew out of the back door, and Kelly got out of driver seat, and check on Rick, let me check you out, and you looks fine, no bite mark. Good, that is relief, about a second later; Kelly got back started up the ambulance, and drove away. Then Rick started to cough and then Kelly realizes that she gave a tainted shot. Then Rick said I am not feeling that well what have you done? Nothing I gave you got you sick it must been something out there got in the wood, but did you eat anything out there, yes but it a grape.

What, I don't understand; I told you not to eat anything, because it is air, no it what you gave me. Then Kelly didn't pay attention and decided to go to Texas, and Rick said where we are going south. Oh I sees, but I think you should go back to Manhattan, no we are going south, but looks there are too many zombies, but I need keep driving, good, I am but once they got into the middle of the zombies, then Rick got up and threw out a dynamite, and blow a few zombies away, and at that moment, he almost slide out but Kelly stop and pull him back, and then the snow was falling and Rick said, hope that we won't end up having a ice storm. But looks fine and nothing, but five zombies got inside and Rick kick him off and Kelly help him with the fight and Rick stab into the skull and blood dripping out the head. Then Kelly and Rick pull them out and threw them into the bushes and mores would coming, and then once again he threw the diamantine and them they will be into bit, and I like that's so do I.

Kelly I just have one more stick of the diamantine and I think it will not be enough and then when into sleep and she didn't hears him speaking, and then Kelly stop and check on him, and he was not breathing, and she did CPR on him and no response, and now what should I do?

He is no waking up so I need to use the equipment and maybe I can save him ands I am doing my best and it still not working and then Kelly did it again and she got his heart going and then Kelly was glad that he was alive, but she looked into his eyes and they were not the same,, and now Kelly think that he will turn into a zombie and why did I save him that I will need to killed him again, and I will not like it, and I will have no choice and I hate this, and then he started to talked and then he said I don't feel the same, but I just want you just let me go! I cannot, you are not zombie, But you what the conclusion will be that you will have to killed me, let me go now, no I think that antidote is working, you are laying to me. No I am not.

When Kelly was helping Rick the Zombies storm them and now Kelly check the doors and windows and make sure that they were not get inside, and the radio was on and the "special report" please stay inside for your own good, there are many infection peoples roaming the streets, and Kelly said I will get us out of here,, but I don't know if I can make it alone. You will and you are a strong woman and you will make it, you are sure about yourself, yes I am, we both will make it, not sure, be sure I need you, but the signs were not good with the blood coming out of his mouth and from his eyes, and then Kelly said " I am sorry what I am about what to do" and she stab him with a the knife that he had in his pocket and Kelly stab him in the head and then he was gone and Kelly started to cried.

HUMANS AND ZOMBIES

Kelly started up the ambulance and kept Rick in the back and knew that he was gone and were not harm her in no way and so she drove through and kept driving in the back roads and was crying so loud and was about screaming and yelling and why am I losing so many friends of mine? But why? I don't want to be alone. About ten miles down the road, there was jeep and she stops and looks around and then a guy name Lenny came out and said and looks into her eyes and said well here is a another zombie to killed, and Kelly said wait a minute, oh you speak, yes I am not one of them, I am human, no kidding, I was going to shoot you with my gun but glad that you spoke, thanks for not killing me, your welcome!

Then he said who that corpse is that in back? Well his name is Rick and he just got infection by eating grape in the woods and he help me to kills some zombies and then he passed out and then I did CPR and then he became a zombie and I just stab his skull and then he is dead, are you sure? Yes I am and the procedure is next to burn him with the rest of the zombies. I cannot do this right now, I just loss him, sure but I will do it. Kelly walks away and then she saw more peoples, and who are they well we survive the virus and so we are a group that killed off the zombies, and we have a battle, and I think you bought a few back on the ways, and we have gun powder, that is great, but I need to be alone for awhile for the losing him, sure don't go too far, I won't.

Later that night the group surrounded the bon fire and the bodies were burned and Kelly said let me says good bye and then hold his hand and said goodbye my dear friend, I thought we were be on going on a long journey but somehow you got sick and became a zombie, sorry my friend, and they toss him into the fire, and he was burned into a crisp.

That night Kelly cried and Lenny came closer to her and hold her and gave her a hug and said you will be fine, I know I will been fighting since 2006 and so far I am not dead, but I just did and so I am not such a good shooter, well you will when they comes forward you, sure, and April said leave my man alone, and Lenny said well stop being jealousy, have no reason too be. Fine and she walks away and then said I will be waiting for you at the tent, fine, well I don't have no place to sleep, don't worry we will find a spot for you, okay! But Kelly kept on the watch of the zombies, but didn't let her guard down and Lenny was looking out for her and April was having a problem with Kelly and told her to leave the camp and Kelly was about do it, and Lenny stop her and said don't listen to her and she will cool off, how do you know, well been dating her for awhile and sometime she could be a bitch. You don't says, but that is the truth, well I am all alone and hope that I am not hitting on you and I just need a place to stayed, that alls, I will explains to her, but she should know that we need to deal with the undead and not with you.

Then Kelly said they are coming and looks out and April is in the ways of the zombies and we cannot shout out, because sounds bring them here and that is not good, what sounds, like the air raid and the sirens, that make them comes and attack us, so hide in the bushes and I will tried to pull April, and Kelly said well I can help you to do a diversion,, no you don't have too, well I need to save her, okay! But April said I could have shoot that zombie, it was a easy shot, well it was but I didn't wants you too get hurt, well you do love me? Yes I do and then Ben came and said what going on mores zombies are coming!!! Yes I sees them and then Kelly was introduce to Ben and said nice too meet you, same here.

Then the guns were shooting at the zombies and there were a lot missing and said Kelly you must be out of practice, well I am not I shot about thousand zombies and I think that you are just bragging about it and I don't believe you, and about ten zombies were about to venous him and Kelly shot the zombie right in the middle of the forehead and he just drop to the floor and Kelly said, I didn't miss any shot, it was April and then April said we were better off went you were not here, thanks for the warm welcome, and Kelly walks away and April gave Lenny a kiss on his lips, and Lenny was a bit angry with April being such bitch. But then Kelly walks away and then April follows her and said why don't you just leave we don't have enough foods and water to feed you, well I still have some spam and some water and don't worry I won't cut into your supplies, and I think that you like my boyfriend think that you cute but I am going stop him and I am not letting him to go and sees what happened I have no interest in your boyfriend., I don't believe it, I think that you are a tease, no I am not and I am scientist, well you are smart pant, what?

I don't need this negative bad mouth whore around here, well I just sees you and then April hit Kelly her nose and Kelly fell down to the ground and Lenny ran over and said what did you do? April and she said this bitch wants you don't you know that we have enough problem with the zombies and lay off with this girl, I am no girl and I am woman, sure you are, and Kelly got up and wipe her nose and when to Ben and said I don't belong here and I will leave in the morning, are you crazy, I am not welcome here, but April has too many issues to deal with and don't pays any attention with her, but she does get wild and crazy in her head and get crazy idea about Peoples and she losing focus and that is bad especially with the zombies situation, no kidding and she so close being killed I know, but that the first time, well, good to know, yes.

Meanwhile, Kelly sat with Ben and talks all night and the Lenny said who will keeps watch tonight, well Ben volunteer, and said well I will helped him out, and April said well you will just distract him, no I will not and then Kelly said looks out there are like a hundred of zombies coming and Kelly started to fires and miss and said she is wasting our bullets, well so do you and we should banned you out of our camp too? No!

The zombies were coming from the woods from alls direction and Kelly said behind you, yes and I got it and looks Lenny,, be careful this zombie is too close to conform. And I know but I am lucky so far, yes you are said Lenny to Kelly and I think this location is not secure and not safe anymore, why do says that to Kelly, well we are in the open and they sees us one point, yes but we need to move immediately, yes and said Ben and Lenny and April said I am not going, what I don't understand, you wants to be dead meat? No but I just want too killed these bastard to hell, but you are taking a risk for the group too. No I am not. But Kelly said let move it and April said well your new friend is a coward and your going to take her advice, so head and I will beat them alone, what do think that you can shoot them and not miss the shot, well I am quality and I know that I can kick ass, and you Kelly you just wants to run and hide, no I don't I wants to save lives, but especially your own of course, and you are selfish, no I am not but you are April and April wanted to comes up to Kelly and hit her face, and Lenny stop her, stop acting like a child, thanks, Kelly putting my boyfriend against me, well you are not me. Then Kelly said I am not going to play your games so I am leaving in my ambulance and you could comes and you can stay and I am not going to force anyone and then Ben and Lenny jump in and said Kelly just keeps on driving and about April doesn't wants to go and she is on her own., well I don't like that, she has to comes, and I am letting her dies, that is not insane. Well she is a bit crazy and does not take order and does the opposite, but carry her and them I will leave, now you are giving me order yes,, we don't want to be slaughter here, I don't neither, so pick her up and carry her here, so how many times to do have to tell you, yes I am going. But hurried I am but then April started to run around and then Lenny caught her and put her inside and she was screaming and yelling. Stops screaming, they will hears you, but be silent, I am said April said the problem is Kelly, before she came it fine, but keep on driving, but not into a tree, I won't I am watching the road, yes, now we need to focus where we are going? Well far away from zombies, yes and we need to stay out of there ways, I agree and then we can just breeze in and out of the city, you think that going to be easy, I don't think so., those zombies have the smell of humans and I don't wants to be the target, I don't neither, well I don't know what do, well drive, and shut up and I don't want to have a collision and die in a crash, I don't want to be alive and beat those zombies, me too, said Kelly but meanwhile April struggle to get free from the zombies, and then Ben said we need to go back to April and save her, are you nuts? No but she will become a zombie, I know that but it is not our control, but still she is our friend, yes that true and she were not leave us behind, yes I don't want you too give me a guilt trip, but you should hear it or not. Shut up and I don't want to hear your voice again, fine but she was our friend and seem like we betray her.

THE WALKING DEAD

Do you sees them coming, yes and I and you are not moving, I don't wants them to spot us, if I move fast they might, sees us and then they will comes for us and that is true, but we cannot stand here and we need to go now, yes but don't make a sound I won't and then somehow April was still yelling and screaming and they went toward April and Kelly said is she some kind fool, make the zombies go toward your ways and I think that she might be suicide, I think she like to be a little dangerous and don't think before she think, that I agree and I know she is not a stupid person but she is, a bit life risking chances and that might be good in someway and some it might not, I know but. But someway she is a diversion and will help us to escape but we need to rescue her, but taking the risk and not making it, I don't think so, well I think that by leaving her that more dangerous, when she become a zombie, she will follow us and shown the other zombies to follow her and that is deadly. I know what you are saying and I think that you should just grab her and take her with us and I don't want to be the one gets blame that I killed your girlfriend, well she make the decision and she decided to stay and fight them and we didn't tell us, I know what you are saying but still get her, or I will.

Meanwhile April was going around in circle and almost fell and then one of the zombie was going to bite her head and then Kelly came and shot the head and the zombie was dead and then numbered grow and Kelly said that we are in deadly territory and we should go now.

But Ben and Lenny said to Kelly and April it is time to go and should not waste a moment and should just keep on walking and stopping for anyone and Kelly said you are right and you should keep us on track and not being lost in the woods, well I know the ways out but I don't want to be ambush by the zombies, I don't neither and they kept walking and running into more of the zombies and Kelly was shooting fast and then Kelly said I cannot do it alone and you need to help me out. Ands Lenny said I will watched you back and you do the same for me, and Kelly said sure, I will, and April said sound like your kissing ass and you wants us to like you and I don't like you or trust her, and Ben said you got us in this jam and Kelly got us out and that the thanks! That you give to Kelly saving your ass and your life, well I would got out alive but you just inference and you got lucky and so now my friends are bragged that you are such a hero but you are not, I were walks out alone, sure next time I will just leave you in the wilderness and I would been okay! Stop talking you giving me a bad headache and I will just walks in front of you and I will search for the walkers that might be lurking out the bushes, well you probably will bring them right too us, well I am the one that alert them, you did, with you genuine idea, thanks, you think that I am smart, so humor yourself, and don't be so sarcasm, well I don't want to be around this bitch, well cool down, April., you going out of control. I thought you were my boyfriend and you stand up for Kelly, because she knows what going on and do you? Not exactly when the killing strain came., a lot persons got sick and they came back to lives and then what they wanted brains.

The only of killing them is by shooting them in the head, watched out I sees of them coming toward us, get down and don't let that zombie sees us, duck down and hide in the bushes and what are you going to do? Don't mind me but I do have a plan, well your plan do backfire and I advice you too come back, no I need to do this, well your stubborn will get you killed, no it will not and I will killed those bastard. Well you use big word and no action, well I know that I will survive this ordeal, and you will thanks me, looked out they are coming, and then Kelly started to blast them and they were falling one by one but she didn't sees the one in back of her and Lenny and Ben were trying to warns her, but she didn't hears them, and then about a minute later, April was dead meat for the zombies and Ben said I need to save her and Kelly said that is too late for her. Kelly hold Ben back and he wanted to fight with Kelly and Kelly said no you cannot do this, she is dead and she will wake up and be a zombie., I know what you saying, but I need to sees her, I cannot let you go Ben, well I wants too but you will happen to you too.

No, It will not and let me go, fine it is your life, yes it is and I will just says goodbye to her, and then I shoot her in head, but you will attract more zombies and we will be stuck here,. No you and Lenny leave and I will catch up with you, I don't like that idea too ,much and you risking your life because you wants to killed your girlfriend, well now she became a zombie, well I did let her go there, well yes but I cannot disagree with your method, well you only live once and so that alls I will says about this, fine and Kelly and Lenny left Ben alone to get rid of April, because she was infection with the deadly infection and that were spread and mores zombies population would grow,. And so that why he had to killed her, had no choice in the matter and then they started to walk and walks and then they heard the gun when off and then Kelly said soon he will be coming soon and I cannot wait to sees my buddy, I agree and we should not separate again, do you hears what I am saying, we need to wait for Ben but not to long and make sure that there are no more sighing of zombies, yes, wait a minute I hears some crackling sound and it must be Ben coming, and then Kelly said I sees him and get yours stuff and we just move on before dark, and we should put up ours tent about a miles away from here, yes and I will do watched, and Lenny said I will do the second watched, fine, do you hearing the moaning and groaning in the woods, and I hears " we wants brains" but where is Ben? Good question, he should be here and I thought he was in back of us, but be alert, I am, I am only seeing zombies, he must be trapped, I think he is.

Kelly said I am going back for him and you watched my back, I will.

Kelly slowly walks through the woods and whisper his name and not a sound from Ben and then Lenny somehow yelled out and said Kelly where are you? I told you not to make a sound and you did, I cannot trust you and in this case you were alert the zombies our ways and I don't have the energy to fight them, do you hear what I am saying too you, comes with me and search for Ben, okay and I won't be a ass anymore, but you are. But Kelly said you need to be quiet and hope that your friend is okay, I hope so. But slow down and we don't want to make a sound, silent.

Okay, I see the path and then I we will go toward the house I think that we are going the wrong ways, no I am not, you are going the wrong direction, I think that I hears him screaming and yelling. That could be the zombies so we need to check it out, fine, it your neck, and mine. Then Lenny fell to the ground and then Kelly pick him up and said, watched your steps and I think there were some woods in the path, I see him and Lenny wave to him but he is not seeing us. Hope that he facing us, and that why we don't have to scream to him.

Lenny was about to sneak up and then Kelly said, wait until I tell you which ways, I wants to sees if he is not infection. Well Lenny when up to him and said Kelly run and run, and but why he is has the strain, what? Then Lenny shot him in the head, well and then ran away and caught up to her and then Kelly said did you get bitten, no I didn't, good. So what ways should we go now, take a left and then a right up the hill and keeps running and don't stop for anything, do you hears? Yes, I do. Suddenly Kelly stop and looked around and said I sees a boat house and we can stay the night there, yes and we need to lock it up good, yes. Follow me and we will be fine and then we can go in the morning and then we can found a car and then walks be safe, and we will not be seen by the zombies. Yes, I agree, with you. But where so between the bushes and hide there and when I get the car and we both can escape the walker and find a safe house for the night, I thought we were going to stay at the boathouse but right now I don't think that is such a good idea, well it were be trapped house and we were be goner, well I don't that's!

There are too many walkers all around us and I don't like this situation and it will not easy to gets out of here, I know that but they are coming toward us at all directions and that is extremely dangerous, well you don't says, it is true,, and I don't know what we are going to do? Well I think that we are just going to sneak out and not being seen, yes and then we will run like you never did before, good plan, went we get there, you will start up the car and drive out so fast that you will not blink, got it.

But stay close too me, I will and don't worry, I will behind you, sure, yes did I ever lies, I don't know you, how were I know, sees walkers they are very near us and they can touch us and then they will bite us. Well you could be right so don't agree with me, okay I won't missy, stop calling me missy.

Don't make a sound, Lenny, I will try not too, if you do they will gets you.

WALKERS, EVERYWHERE WE TURNED

Lenny looks they are behind you and just be quiet and they will not hear you, but they will smell me and then I will be "dead meat" no don't says that's but it is true, I don't wants to hears that from your mouth, do you hear me? Yes but they hears us too, don't realized that we are a target of there food chains and then we are dealing with chaos and zombies wanted to eat our brain that is disgust, to what you are saying, but you better move your ass, you will be caught by that ugly creature of the zombie. You are too close and I that zombie has his eye on you, no he does and don't get paranoid I am not but we are not fighting them off but we don't have a weapon, use your bow and arrow, well aim toward the head,, got it and don't miss it, and don't let them sees us, well you are such bossy broad, well I am trying to stay alive.

Looks out, looks out, you are just like few inches apart of the zombie and he can catch you, move over toward me, but don't sees on the crowds of the walker, oh my god, huh! Now we are in doodle, what? We are goner, no, we are not we need to jump over the car and just a few of them but we will be following, no shit we will, I will speed away and then what end up in a ditch and then they can swallow us, no thanks! That kind of getting away is too crazy and suicide and I don't like it, well we just can sit here and be ate up, that no way of dying, and it will be a sunny day tomorrow, if we make it tonight, I have no doubt but we will, I promise you, you cannot promise me anything. I won't listen to you but we are going out here, but seems like you are sure of yourself.

One hour later went the zombies were about to stomp on Lenny and Kelly. Kelly lit some fire and put on some music toward the old truck and make a diversion and then we will escape and some firecrackers and lit the skies.

That sound a good idea and I will run and get into the car and drive back to you. Yes but don't leave, you don't trust me? I do but this time you just think of staying alive. I know. They are coming out the bushes and they are climbing on the car and they will smash the window and they will get inside, and they will takes and I won't let them., you will not have no control and they will killed us, stop it. I cannot, they are surrounded us and we are block and now what? Well I don't know but we just cannot sit here, go now, but it wont started., I feel that we are jinx, no we are not and you are superstition, and you gets too scare too quickly, but they are coming from the barn and they are coming from the woods and from the ground, now what? I don't know what to do? Looks out one zombie jump in the front of the car try to toss him off and I don't wants that zombies to crack the window and grab me., well I probably will be the first one to go! Don't says that it could happen, but we will be out of the zombies zone and they are not that strong and they walks very slow but the strength is strong and then Kelly said don't you sees that they are eating gut and kidney and livers and brains., and that body is torn into bit and the blood is splatter, yes and I am going to drive around them, good and I don't want to get stuck here, I don't neither. But I need to tells you that we will be running out gas and the rest of the ways we need to walks and we will have to walks fast., but where are going to stay, I am able to walks that far and I feel that my ankle is in pain, well maybe I can found you a stick. But find a thick stick and like a crutch, yes I will but we will do about half mile to go, great! But Kelly didn't like that they might be doom because Lenny does not know how to navigation the ways and seem like he is going in circle, and the place the same,, and more zombies heading toward us and now I want to shoot but I cannot really aim. But Lenny was just driving and then the car stall and then Kelly said well I guess we need to step out of the car and I think that we should just hike through the path and do think so? Yes I know. You know what? Well I am not exactly sure. But I believe that we will be fine, okay, if you says so, I am. Good, I am not sure that we will be clear from the zombies and maybe going right at them. stop this, you are making me sick and the sirens when off and they were coming and now I knew it was time to run and run for our life.

About a minute, Kelly said there is a little boy and he looks like he is scare so should I grab him? Do you think that he is fine? Not sure but we need to help him and the little boy was sitting on the grass and crying and

Kelly was going to get him and then the walkers came and caught him., and Lenny said you walk too slow, and now he is gone, you knew that my ankle in pain and you could prevent his death. But Lenny, you would be trigger happy, no I am yes you are. But Kelly walk away, and Lenny follow her and it was really bad and blood was flowing. But then you have kind of symptom, well you are drooling, and some vomit. Yes but it is not the virus, I don't want to become a zombie, then the zombies dash out trying out and pulling out and torn into pieces, then I don't want to be chew up, and I am running. Ands then he fell down hurt his arm and she pick him up him and they both ran. Kelly we have no place to hide, so let go inside here for awhile, okay. Then we will leave, yes. About one hour later, they heard trucks and they looks around there two men that wouldn't zombies, they pull out the gun, and they started to shoot, they fell to the ground. But they wouldn't zombies but why they shoot them, and Lenny said well, they would going to shoot us and we would end of dead.

But how do you know he was going killed us, and you don't feel remorse, no, this is the world that we are living, a danger one, I know and I am going to dies, then they heard sound and doors would being lock, and what are you saying? They closing us in here, we will be able to escape, I think we will, through the vent. Will be big enough, to get through, but it be tight, don't have doubt, I don't but you sees them watching the doors and windows and having a sniper on the roof, if we try to step out and we will gets shot into our head, no we are not, we will make it. believe we need to tells them that we not infection and we are dead, and we do not eat flesh, but they will be shooting at us, and they killed us and we lay next to the zombies on the floor, it is not going happen. What are you saying we have to stay low, and silent, about a minute later, Lenny felt a hand on his leg, and said stop touching me, I am not. Your not who is? He turned around it was a zombie, hold on don't let it bite, it was about to drag him, Kelly pointed the gun and shoot in the head, and Lenny said my ears are hurting from the blast, thanks! I did, what? I don't hear you, what? You really blast that zombie, and now I am having a bad effective of the gunshot. But keeps coming and we need of moving, yes I am but would be safe, I don't know. About a second the building was shaking and the walls were falling down and we will be bury alive in this building, and no one will looks for us, I think that you are right! I didn't want you do agree with me, we have the soldiers in the front of the building and then we have zombies inside and no really escape neither ways we will get shot, no we are not, and we will not become zombie, you don't know anything, yes I do, I am surviving and so are you and don't give up on life, I been in this battle since 7 years and I did lose the battle so far you been lucky, luck has nothing to do with it, you need to know what you are doing and lives and don't let the living dead catch you and infection, you totally right about that's! by not giving up, we will gets out of here and they will not shoot us. It not today or tomorrow we will walks out of here, in one piece. So they walks slowly and then we will underneath and then climb to the second floor and then try to squeeze out of the window.

Looks there one soldier is about to shoot at us, and I need to tells him, that I am the general daughter, but your father got killed and I think this time it not going to work, I need to tells that I am the scientist that work on the antidote, not will not works neither because, the result, were not good they alls turned into zombies., that sure but they should sees, that I am the one that make it. they will shoot and asked questions later, and you will be dead, I advice you not too, fine. But I need to try, and Kelly spoke out and the bullet flew in front of her, and miss her by a inch, that was really close.

But they think that we are infection and it is not going to work., stop saying that's! fine. Listens, do you hears anything, no I don't looks what happening, they are getting slaughter by the zombies. they are a going to get inside and we will get slaughter too.

Now you are sounding like me, no kidding, you are, I don't wants to hears that from you. But Kelly yelled out and Lenny pull out of the window and spotted the Zombie that was going to bite her, and then said you save me. Yes I did, give me a kiss, no I am not. Why not? This could be the end, no way, I am going fight with my last breathe, it is a possibility you will. Comes out with me, you will knock him down and then I will but the knife right into his skull and then it will died, good plan, and I wander how many are there, I do not sees the soldiers they must be wipe out, your right! That is a bad sign, yes it is, the sirens were going out and they saw thousand of zombies on the street, and I think we should stay here, there is no place to go, I think that you are. And looked out and the soldiers were alls dead and the heads and feet and bodies part shatter all over the street and one eating the brain, and pulling it out of the head, and eating it.

It is so gross and I cannot looks at it, but you must looks what going on, I know the virus spread and the contagion got worst, yes that is the scenario that we are dealing right, and don't let them sees you, but they do sees us, go back inside and seem like they are going to break in, hope not. Just listens to the sound, and they are crashing in and they wants us and we need to hide, and yes but I think we need more bullets and then Kelly notice that there was helicopter and said this is our escape, do you know how to fly the copter? Yes I do and I need to shown you, but looks there are few near the copter, and the gun somehow didn't fire, and it got stuck and they were coming toward them, and run downstairs.

But we are block and we have no ways to go, yes we do, need to go to the basement and then out of that window, yes. But they are close with steel and other stuff and we are unable to open it, so we need to find hammer and then we can bang it out and hope to keep them out, I am praying for ours lives. But we will be able to escape and not be in any quarantine, that is right, and being in this situation gets worst. Yes it does, and I don't like it at alls. But you need to know that I will squeeze out and make the opening bigger, yes but we need to gets some guns from the dead soldiers, and put some smelly death on us, yes, and hope it does not rain, don't talked about rain, especially acid rain that make it worst, I didn't know that's! now you do and I don't like it, quiet, I am about to stick out my head, and it looks safe so far, and I going to climb out and get one of the jeep and we can drive out from here. Hope it works, I think that it will work, I am in back of you, good and I will follow where you go.

This moment is very danger, that I will do., and if they smell me, I will be a goner, I know that, and I know that you will be okay! Then one shot was fire, and Kelly had to go back inside and we are not exactly clear we still need to deal with zombies and military, yes and we still could died here. No, go and run, and the shooting didn't stop and then Kelly was hit in the shoulder and she was bleeding, and Lenny said hold it tight, and it will stop, but I am in bad pain and my wound is open, save yourself, Lenny.

No, I am not going to leave you and I am going to comes out and you are going to get shot, I don't care at this point, well, you should and maybe your family is still alive, well right now you are my family and I am going to bring you back, no you should somehow get yourself in the jeep and leave me., never, I won't! about five minutes later Lenny was climb out of the window and looks around and stay down and make sure that he were not get shot, and Kelly said around the corner there is a sniper on the roof, and I think that you are very near to the jeep. But the soldiers order would too shoot anyone that was walking, and then Kelly and Lenny, they got inside and hide and they are throwing smoke bombs and they wants us to comes out, whatever you do cover your face., yes I will use the face mask and we will not get infection and looks they are going start a fire, no they won't, yes they are, we will burns, so I says that we should just get the hell out of here, no! comes with me, no I am scare and I just don't want to go, well you prefer to stay here and died, no. it just pitch black, and we are in the middle of the battle, great scenario, yes it is. But I think someway we can just go out a different ways,, don't you understand that we are quarantine, and there is no escape, there is always, tell me, and I am going to listens to you, what is the plan, I am thinking, well so far I have nothing, okay! WE are in quarantine, and we are not leaving, not now but maybe later. But we are still in quarantine and no escape, stop this, I don't want to hear this anymore., leave me alone, fine. Lenny walks away toward the door and a shot was fire but it misses him by an inch.

THIN ICE ZOMBIES IN LA
NOWHERE TO RUN OR HIDE!

QUARANTINE PART 1

ABOUT THE AUTHOR

Jean Marie Rusin, live with her mom and brother in New Britain, CT, and Jean Marie Rusin, graduation from Connecticut School of Broadcasting, On September 7, 2007, Jean Marie Rusin, has my own talk radio show, on www. Blogtalkradio.com and Jean Marie Rusin, member to Connecticut Authors and Publishers, and I am on Face book and Jean Marie Rusin Fan Club, CT and Jean Marie Rusin Fan Club (Michigan) and Moon Eclipse Days of Darkness, Book Club, on Face book, and now twitter and www. Myspace.com. my website is www. Jeanmarierusin. com